THE KREMLIN WATCHER

Also by Will Perry

MURDER AT THE UN

The
Kremlin Watcher

A NOVEL OF SUSPENSE BY

WILL PERRY

DODD, MEAD & COMPANY, NEW YORK

1   2   3   4   5   6   7   8   9   10

Library of Congress Cataloging in Publication Data

Perry, Will.
    The Kremlin watcher.

    I. Title.
PZ4.P467Kr   [PS3566.E722]   813'.5'4   78–1428
ISBN 0–396–07529–0

1

Stefan held the phone away from his ear as if it were red hot, and stared out of the back window. His uncle's farm stretched as far as the highway, not another house in sight, but he didn't notice any of it. His mind was back in Warsaw, carefully calculating what he should do now—how long he might have left. How stupid to think he could get away, even for a weekend!

"Stefan, are you there? Isn't it great news?"

His sister's voice, faint, distant, sounded so happy; he envied her simple reaction.

"What did you say?"

"Are you drunk, Stefan? Have you been drinking Uncle Frédéric's homemade vodka?"

"No, I was just thinking about it. The news . . . I didn't expect it."

"Nobody did. People here are already celebrating."

"I'll get an early train back." Dober would want to see him, would want some explanation of why he'd missed it.

"You don't sound so happy, Stefan."

"It's a great day for Poland," he said, "if there isn't some trick behind it." He couldn't tell her his real reaction; he wasn't sure how much she knew.

"I'll meet you at the station."

He went outside to tell his uncle. The old man was on the

1

other side of the field, sitting upright on his tractor as if it were a horse. His family had farmed this land outside Poznan for over a century and had grown used to the ebb and flow of invaders. For the last forty years it had been one long continuous occupation, first by the Germans and then by the Russians; but everything had an end, his uncle was fond of saying, except the land.

The soft earth still felt strange underfoot to Stefan. He crossed the field in his worn city shoes, breathing in the clear country air as if sampling a new drink; it was cold in his polluted lungs. This weekend in the country had seemed a good idea back in Warsaw. He'd come hoping to clear his head, to find a way out of the double life he was now living. But the phone call had brought him not only the big news but the realization he was already too late.

His uncle waved and turned the tractor to meet him. The old man was a little slower, but otherwise was hardly changed from the days Stefan used to run behind him as a boy. Stefan could still remember his uncle's tales about his two great Polish heroes: Copernicus, who as an astronomer had looked "outside" the world, and Chopin, who as an artist had looked "inside." His uncle had been named Frédéric after Chopin. As the old man came across the field, his cheeks still ruddy, his blue eyes sharp and clear, he seemed as comforting, as unchanging to Stefan as a lighthouse to a ship lost in a storm.

"I've got great news!" Stefan tried to sound excited.

His uncle listened closely and then threw back his head and roared with delight. "So they go home at last! Ah, God is good to us."

"The railways and the roads to the frontier are crowded with tanks and soldiers."

"Dreams do come true, Stefan, if you wait long enough— and pray hard enough." The old man was still very religious; he had been angry when he learned that Stefan no longer went to mass. "Why do you think they do it at this time?"

"They must be convinced the government is strong enough."

"Or they got tired of being here?"

They drank vodka to celebrate, and the old man brought out plates of sausages and pickles. Stefan put on such a poor act that his uncle examined him with concern.

"Stefan, you must get more rest." The clear blue eyes ran over his thin face and bony body. "You do not look after yourself. You reporters work too long hours in smoky rooms. You've lost weight; you're a bad color even for someone living in the city. Remember, nothing else matters if we lose our good health."

Or if we lose our life, Stefan thought.

"The news doesn't make you happy, Stefan?"

"Yes," he said, "if they're leaving for good. If it's not some trick."

"Ah," the old man said, "learn to enjoy one step at a time. Nothing is forever, except the earth."

He insisted on giving Stefan food to take with him— enough for several people. "You need building up, Stefan!" On the train, Stefan tried to share it with some children who were watching him hungrily, but their mother wouldn't let them take it. She, too, mustn't have liked the way he looked. He ate a little of the sausage and then put it away for later; he felt too nervous to eat.

Outside Warsaw, the train was kept waiting for half an hour while the Russians went by. He saw the huge, ugly tanks and the broad, young soldiers' faces through the train windows. Yes, it was true enough.

He was met at the station by his sister and Miron, still in his factory overalls. Even the big, taciturn Miron seemed excited. There was to be a secret meeting that night, he said. "Now the Russians are leaving, we can hurry up our plans."

"Why do you think they're doing it?"

3

"We fooled them. They've never understood us."

"You want me to attend the meeting?"

"Of course."

"It's not too risky?"

"Everyone's too busy celebrating."

That's not the point, he thought, but he couldn't tell them. At first he was tense, nervous, constantly looking round for someone following—the Russians or the Americans. But Miron was so cheerful—"They've played into our hands," he said as if he didn't care who heard—that walking outside between them, he began to feel more light-hearted. It was the feeling he had gone to the country for, the feeling of being a simple Pole among Poles again; and a wave of patriotism and camaraderie buoyed him up: a simple faith like his uncle's, but personal not religious.

They got in Miron's car, teasing each other like teenagers. But as he sat back laughing, the mirror suddenly showed him the face his uncle had seen: worn, pinched, furtive—scared. And he was deflated.

The Russians hadn't informed him beforehand and that could only mean they no longer trusted him. He was a threat to them. What could he do about it? He didn't want to die.

At the time the news from Poland was reaching Washington, a high school teacher in New York City named Ursula Rogal was coming out of a psychiatrist's office on the East Side, looking pleased with herself. She hadn't been there for treatment, but for information, and what she'd learned—a name—had opened up new possibilities for her.

A tall, slim, poised woman in her mid-forties, she hesitated outside on the sidewalk, impatient for action. She decided she couldn't wait until she reached home to make a phone call. She had to know *now*. She went into a drugstore and phoned Information for the number. As she made the call, her expression went through several changes: at first pleas-

4

ant, even ingratiating, she soon soured and became almost threatening with the other person. But at the end she looked very satisfied.

Her next stop was at a downtown office building that housed countless small companies and associations, obscure professional groups, and minor labor unions. She took the elevator up to the sixth floor—to a private detective agency, the kind that has one room, one desk, and one ex-city policeman, whose main business is guard duty and divorce work.

A heavily built, balding man glanced up from an old manual typewriter as she entered.

"Miss Rogal, how are ya?"

"How's my case?"

"Nothing for you yet," the man said evasively. "We've got feelers out to all the states and all the South American countries. But that kind of investigation takes time."

"How much time? It's now two years since I hired you."

"It's a big job," he said. "Tryin' to trace a man who disappeared thirty years ago—and in Europe, too. Needle in a haystack." He smiled patiently. "But we never give up until we've cracked the case. Don't worry." He was used to placating clients—and creditors.

"I've already paid you hundreds of dollars in fees and expenses."

"It's costly work covering all those countries, Miss Rogal. International connections cost money . . ."

She had fallen for that line at first; now she didn't believe anything he said. His "international connections" were probably in Brooklyn or the Bronx; he probably didn't even know where Poland was.

"All this time you've found out nothing."

"We know he's in the American hemisphere."

"That's like saying he's in Europe or Asia. I could have guessed as much—many of them made for North or South America. But where?"

5

"Our inquiries are narrowing," he said vaguely.

"I've decided I can't afford you any more."

"Wait a couple of months, Miss Rogal. Just a couple of months more. Then we'll have something for you . . ."

"No, I've waited long enough. I'm going to try another way," she said.

It was her turn to be vague. He wondered if she meant another agency. Except for the money, he wasn't sorry to lose her, and he sensed he'd got as much out of her as he could without trouble. There was something odd about her, something behind her obsessive search that made him uneasy. . . .

She took the subway up the West Side to her apartment. She was now in a restless mood. A cup of coffee, TV—nothing relaxed her. She pulled out a suitcase from under the bed and unlocked it. Inside was an old Nazi SS uniform, pressed and neat. She took it out to air it for her visitor that evening. Perhaps she could persuade him to wear it.

Ursula Rogal had a strange, almost nostalgic expression as she fingered the uniform's black leather belt. . . .

2

The special messenger flew from Washington, D.C., to New York, where a limousine was waiting at Kennedy to drive him to Columbia University. He had no difficulty reaching his destination, a small obscure lecture hall, but then guards barred his way. No one was allowed in without a special pass; not even phone calls were being received. He identified himself and showed the guards the sealed envelope he'd been instructed to deliver personally, and at last, with a guard at his side, he was allowed to enter.

All he knew was that the secret annual convention of kremlinologists—or Kremlin watchers—was being held; in that seedy little hall were the West's foremost experts on the Communist world. Most of them worked for governments, international corporations, universities, or the media.

As he walked down the aisle, peering along the rows of studious faces, he felt like a nonswimmer thrown in at the deep end. Voices, often with heavy foreign accents, were shouting across the hall, making references he couldn't follow. Speakers bobbed up and down, gesticulating at each other. They seemed to be discussing the kremlinologists' current obsession, future relations between the Soviet Union and China, but they might just as well have been talking about computer programming for all the sense it made to him. He gathered there was a big argument in progress, but

7

he couldn't understand what it was all about. Poland seemed to be at the center of it, a country he knew next to nothing about—it was somewhere in eastern Europe, part of the Soviet bloc, but otherwise it was just a name to him.

He spotted the lean man with bushy red hair he was looking for—Mervyn Podz, chief Soviet analyst of the Central Intelligence Agency—sitting near the front, listening closely to a speaker on the other side of the aisle. Everyone, in fact, was concentrating so hard on what the speaker, a small man with a slight foreign accent and large visionary eyes, was saying, that they made way reluctantly, absentmindedly, for him to hand Podz the sealed envelope. Podz himself was so involved that he broke the seal while he continued to listen. Catching the mood, the special messenger turned to listen, too.

". . . the Soviet Union is going to be too busy holding its European empire together to have much time for China. Poland will be the first trouble spot. My analysis of the available facts shows we can expect a workers' uprising in Poland comparable to those of 1956 and 1970, which, you'll recall, brought down the reigning Communist party chiefs in Warsaw. . . ."

The speaker soon lost the special messenger's attention, but it was apparently heady stuff for the assembled kremlinologists—almost as exciting as predicting the winner of a big race. One or two of the younger men gave audible gasps. The special messenger saw Podz shake his head vehemently while he took out a long typewritten report from the envelope and, still half listening, began to read.

The special messenger asked a man with a beard in the next row who the speaker was.

"Leo Farel," came the curt reply, as if he should have known.

The special messenger knew the name from TV. Farel was one of the best known of the independent kremlinologists and analyzed Soviet events on TV news programs and for newspapers, and frequently lectured at universities. Podz's close attention and his hostile attitude were more understandable then; there was always a strong professional rivalry between government kremlinologists and the independents.

As Farel sat down, there was scattered applause—the little man was obviously widely respected. He had even received the highest tribute possible for a kremlinologist: abuse from the Soviet press. *Pravda* had called him "a lackey of Wall Street" many times when he came too close to unpleasant truths.

Podz put the report down slowly and stared triumphantly at Farel. When the applause had stopped, he said loudly across the aisle so everyone could hear, "You're wrong, Leo. There is no conclusive evidence to support your prediction." There was a rumble of agreement from other government analysts. "In fact, the opposite seems to be the truth." Podz held up the report. "News has just reached me that the Soviet Union has begun to withdraw most of its army from Poland." A murmur of astonishment went round the hall. "Would that make sense if any trouble was expected? Our information from Warsaw is that the present Polish government is strong and well supported. The Poles are finding it hard to live with rising food prices like everyone else, but there's no sign of nationally organized protests. Dreams of new uprisings in Poland are—what would you say?—pipe dreams!"

It was a strong, covertly personal attack and heads turned to see how Farel was reacting to it. He sat with folded arms, smiling confidently. "Just wait and see," he said quietly, looking across at Podz. "The Poles may have learned to live with communism, but not with communism *and* inflation."

Podz laughed. "You're wrong this time, Leo. The withdrawal of the Soviet army will please the Poles. The presence of Russian soldiers has been a constant irritant to their pride.

They won't cause any big trouble and risk the Russians coming back. Nobody wants another Hungary or Czechoslovakia. It's a master stroke on the Russians' part."

Most of the other kremlinologists nodded in agreement. A Polish uprising now seemed impossible. Farel was a great analyst, but this time he had gone too far. Yet such was their respect for him that when the convention ended and the kremlinologists dispersed to their various countries, they all kept a careful watch on Poland for several days. But nothing happened. The peaceful situation remained unchanged. The Soviet army completed its evacuation, and gradually Farel's prediction became a joke, a target for barbed academic witticisms. But the kremlinologists were premature. Just two weeks after the convention in New York, the news came. That morning a series of well-organized strikes had begun in factories throughout Poland. By the next day, it was clear this was the beginning of a serious workers' uprising that could overturn the Soviet-backed government.

Leo Farel had been proved right.

3

Only one of the high-backed leather chairs was empty.

Everyone else was there, rustling papers, talking in low voices, waiting anxiously. Several tanned, fleshy faces kept eyeing the door.

The group around the long table resembled a board meeting of a large corporation, waiting for its chairman. One of the men was even an aging military man—every large corporation made room for at least one retired army general. Only these faces were better known than businessmen; they appeared regularly on TV or in the newspapers.

The National Security Council was awaiting the president in the Cabinet Room at the White House. He was flying in from making a speech in Philadelphia and was already a half hour late. Pete Baldwin, the president's special assistant on national security affairs and his intelligence expert, had reported that the president intended to attend, which surprised no one. The news from Poland was said to have infuriated the president, a quick-tempered man at the best of times who drove his staff hard but generally got results—"much better results than this," as he'd told Baldwin with some expletives Baldwin didn't pass on to the members of the NSC.

Not only had he been given no warning about Poland, but he was in the middle of a gruelling re-election campaign. The latest opinion polls showed him and his opponent, Senator

Barker, running neck-and-neck, only one percentage point between them. He wanted a tricky international incident "like I want a hole in the head," he told the secretary of state angrily on the phone from Philadelphia.

The president arrived at last, clutching a bulging briefcase, preceded by Secret Servicemen. It was easy to see he was in a bad temper. His broad, clean-shaven face, pale from weeks of cross-country campaigning, was unsmiling, which was rare, and he didn't acknowledge anyone's greeting. He began speaking almost before he'd sat down.

"Gentlemen, you'll all know by now that we've been taken completely by surprise . . ."

There was a rush to explain it. He listened impatiently to an up-to-date briefing by the director of Central Intelligence, with additional comments by the secretary of state and the chairman of the Joint Chiefs of Staff. He heard a report on the latest developments in Polish industrial towns like Radom, where workers had destroyed the local Communist party headquarters.

"Gentlemen," he snapped at the end, "to put it bluntly, you were all caught with your pants down. You completely misread the Polish situation."

"If it's any consolation," said the director of Central Intelligence, "the Soviet Union misread it, too."

"It isn't any consolation," snapped the president. "Already every goddam Polack in the country is asking what we're going to do about it. It's all I was asked in Philadelphia this morning. My s.o.b. of an opponent has already seized on it as a big issue. If we'd had some goddam warning about it, we could have been prepared."

"When the Soviet army withdrew," the secretary of state said, "the embassy reported—"

"Don't tell me what the goddam embassy reported," the president told him. "They're so busy attending the goddam opera they don't know a goddam thing about what's happen-

12

ing in the Polish factories." He caught the director of Central Intelligence looking pleased at this putdown of his rival, and he turned on him with a scowl. "What the hell were your agents doing? They must have been asleep on the job. Surely to God they've got some worker informers who could have flashed us a warning."

"It was a very skillful operation, kept very secret—"

"Not *that* secret. According to a CBS report I watched on the plane, there was one person who predicted it weeks ago. But he wasn't in this goddam government."

"Leo Farel," murmured the secretary of state.

"How the hell could he—one man!—predict it when you fellers couldn't do it with all the resources of the federal government and a huge budget behind you?"

"Lucky guesswork," the director of Central Intelligence said quickly.

"No," the secretary of state said, "Farel's been right before when we've all been wrong."

"Maybe you should recruit him," the president snapped.

"We've tried."

The president brought his hand down on the table with a bang that shook the glass of iced Coca-Cola beside his briefing papers.

"I don't care how you do it, gentlemen, but I want to know what the Soviet Union now intends to do. Is the Soviet army going back into Poland to crush the revolt, or are they going to stay out and let the Poles settle it for themselves in the best interests of détente and general good relations with the rest of Europe and with us? Maybe the Polish government can handle it alone and weather the storm. But if the Russians are going to make a move, I want to know about it so I can appear to counter it in some way short of war. This could well decide the election." He got up, facing the large map of Poland used in the background briefing. "I want to know as soon as possible, within a day or two, before it's too late."

13

He looked challengingly at the rivals: on one side, the directors of Central Intelligence and the Defense Intelligence Agency—who used to fight over the division of the intelligence budget, but had recently formed an uneasy alliance—and, on the other side, the secretary of state, who was more in favor of détente with the Russians than the other two. It was a sophisticated version of hawks versus doves. But with a strong president, neither side dominated—they competed for his attention. That was the way he liked it: divide the specialists and dominate *them.*

"Don't fail me a second time," the president said, already on his way out.

At the door, the director of Central Intelligence stopped him to whisper—the secretary of state, an amateur violinist who prided himself on his hearing, overheard something about "a top-level Soviet source." He watched the president nod, obviously pleased, and he began to worry. What did the CIA have up its sleeve?

4

Stefan doodled as the briefing at the U.S. embassy dragged on. An earnest young American information officer, new to the game, was announcing the visit of some American orchestra as if it were a radical event. The orchestra's program, he said, would include a Chopin concerto. Of course, Stefan thought cynically, and it would probably be the same Chopin concerto the visiting Soviet orchestra played last week. He was only there to meet Frank Dober, the CIA station chief. While the orchestra's itinerary was read out, he leaned over and picked up an American reporter's copy of *The New York Times.*

"May I?"

"Keep it."

Events in Poland were on the front page, with a picture of workers demonstrating in the streets of Radom. He was surprised to read that, according to the report, the workers' uprising had been predicted weeks before by an American kremlinologist. When he and Dober bumped into each other "by chance" at the end of the briefing, he mentioned it. "Maybe you'd be better off employing him."

"Those backroom boys are always wise after the event," Dober grunted contemptuously. "My worry is how we came to miss it."

Stefan stared sympathetically at the big, gray-haired man

with a military erectness and the kind of middle-aged boyish-
ness that many Europeans still associated with Americans.
He liked Dober and wished he could level with him, but
Dober would never understand. The CIA station chief would
forgive anything done against the Russians but nothing
against his own side; their friendship depended on complete
loyalty.

"I'm driving home, Stefan. Can I drop you anywhere?"

"Yes, thanks. I've got to meet somebody."

They left the embassy, casually chatting; nobody seemed
even to notice. Their casual association wasn't suspicious:
Dober's cover at the embassy was the political section and
it was natural he would be on friendly terms with local
journalists, especially a free-lancer like Stefan, who didn't
work for any one paper.

Dober drove carefully through the busy streets. It was
business as usual as far as possible. A roadblock and a group
of workers marching with homemade banners were the only
signs of the troubles.

"Washington wants to know why we missed it," Dober
said as they passed the workers. "After you returned from
Poznan, didn't you hear any whispers?"

Stefan shook his head irritably. He was tired of being
asked about it, tired of lying. "How's your wife?" he asked
quickly as a diversion.

Dober immediately bristled. "She's fine," he said, his eyes
narrowing, watchful.

Damn, Stefan thought, I touched a sensitive spot there. He
added smoothly, "You both must have dinner with me some
time."

"We shouldn't be seen too much together," Dober said
irritably. Then his attitude suddenly softened. "But a dinner
sometime, that wouldn't be suspicious. Not if my wife came
along." He smiled, more friendly. "I get your point."

16

Stefan was safe now. No more questions. "Let me out here, Frank." He added casually, "I'm meeting one of the Russians—at his request. The excuse is background information for *Pravda*. I guess they want to find out if I know anything they don't."

"I know about the meeting," Dober said.

"I thought you would."

Dober said earnestly, "If you learn what they intend to do . . ." He stopped as if embarrassed.

"Of course," Stefan said, surprised, "I'll let you know immediately."

When he got out of the car, Dober suddenly followed him. They stood in the street staring at each other. Stefan had an uneasy feeling Dober knew more than he should, otherwise why was he acting so strangely?

Stefan was right: Frank Dober did know something, but not what Stefan thought.

The CIA station chief stared at Stefan's pinched, familiar face, the bright eyes and sallow skin, and he felt a great urge to tell him the truth—to save his life. They had worked together a long time; Stefan trusted him, the fool. Dober had to call on all his powers of self-control to keep quiet. What could he say that wouldn't give it away?

"Stefan . . ."

Stefan looked expectant. He seemed to sense something.

Dober held out his hand. It was a mistake, he usually didn't do that, but he wanted to make some gesture.

Stefan hesitated and then shook hands. "We are becoming formal."

Dober shrugged. "Someone might be watching."

Stefan grinned. "Very un-Polish, old buddy. Well . . . goodbye then," Stefan said and then paused as if reluctant to leave. He must feel something.

17

Something casual was needed to end it. "See you . . . tomorrow." Dober found the lie hard—he, a veteran at the game.

"Okay, Frank," Stefan said. "I'll phone you."

Then Stefan was walking away, past a little Polski Fiat taxi waiting for someone—unless it was a cover for watching them—past one of the interminable lines outside a new Western-style supermarket. Stefan's slight shabby figure blended easily with the men and women in heavy topcoats and woollen scarves waiting impatiently in the cold. Although the workers were forcing concessions from the now shaky government, the meat queue was still a fact of life in Warsaw.

He wanted to call Stefan back, there was still time. But he couldn't afford to, and he watched Stefan approach the end of the street where he'd disappear into an almost certain trap. He was sacrificing an old colleague, an old buddy, to protect someone who meant nothing to him personally, but was a more valuable source. If he warned Stefan, if he shouted to him now to stop, the Russians would know where the information had come from, and Ivan's cover would be blown.

Frank Dober watched helplessly as Stefan went round the corner, out of sight. Then, aware that he was conspicuous, he got back into the car, his face strangely bitter. Doctors must feel this way after talking to patients who don't yet know they're going to die, Dober told himself.

He waited for news all evening. He was snappy with the children—he had a boy of four and a girl of three—and they kept away from him. His wife wanted to get a babysitter and go to a movie, but he told her he had a headache. She knew something was wrong, but she never questioned him, and he didn't feel like talking; it was probably safer for her to know nothing—nothing at all. She was his second wife, fifteen years younger, and sometimes he worried that he overprotected her, but some things she couldn't know. The Agency had wanted him to leave her behind in the States, but

18

you couldn't risk that with a young wife. Every young jock in D.C. would have been after her. It was bad enough in Warsaw with the Poles. There had been a time when he suspected there was something between her and Stefan. Stefan wasn't much to look at, but women liked him.

He said casually, watching her closely, "I bumped into Stefan at the embassy."

"How is he?" She sounded unmoved, her eyes on the TV. He let it drop.

At last the news came; it was all confirmed in a brief phone call from an informer at police headquarters. Stefan had been found in a field on the outskirts of the city, shot in the back.

Dober poured himself a glass of Scotch and drank it straight while his wife pretended to watch TV. She kept glancing at him. Finally he told her Stefan was dead, without the details.

"How did it happen?"

"The police are investigating."

Suddenly she got up and hurried from the room, and he thought he could hear her sobbing in the bathroom. All his damnable suspicions came back. Later, in bed, she whispered they ought to leave Poland; what had happened to Stefan might happen to him; she worried about it constantly. Gradually his suspicions subsided, and he wondered if the paranoia of the job was seeping into his marriage. What did it matter anyway now Stefan was dead? He remembered the Polish journalist as he'd last seen him, passing the queue of shoppers, disappearing. Stefan was too high a price to pay! Ivan had better come through now with what Washington wanted . . .

They met in Warsaw's restored old quarter in a church that was a star of all the Warsaw guidebooks, a genuine Polish relic, one of the few that had survived the Nazis.

Dober arrived first, and the atmosphere oppressed him;

19

dust and stale incense amid the ancient statues and crucifixes and other symbols of Catholic ritual. Catholicism was foreign to him, an American Baptist by birth, a Nothing by adult choice; and Polish Catholicism was doubly foreign, a retreat to the past in this Communist country. Yet up to seventy percent of the population was said still to attend weekly services; one active Communist party member had recently confided to a CIA informer that he sent his young son to mass not for religious reasons "of course," but so that the boy could understand the realities of Polish life and a thousand years of Polish history. This strange, uneasy Catholic-Communist relationship explained the ambivalence of the country's position in the Soviet empire—and also much of the present tension, because Catholic leaders had backed the workers against the official Communist ideology and made Soviet suppression much more difficult.

Two old women were lighting candles, otherwise the big drafty old church was empty. Dober sat close to the wall on the left side facing the altar, ten rows from the back—Ivan's instructions had been admirably precise. Dober was in semi-darkness, a shadow among shadows. The old women, crossing themselves and gossiping over the candles, were not even aware he was there. They chuckled and talked loudly enough for him to hear a few Polish words about food prices and somebody's husband. They helped to lessen the effect of the religious symbolism and mysticism that made Dober so uneasy. He would have been more relaxed at a Communist party meeting than in this church simply because the Communists shared his pragmatic, political approach, even if their aims were different.

One of the side doors opened; Dober glanced back quickly. No, it wasn't Ivan; it was only a teenage girl in a shabby raincoat with a fur collar, shy and nervous as if afraid of being seen. The old women stopped gossiping long enough to examine her and then started again—something about the recent demonstrations in Radom where one of the old women had relatives . . . The girl crossed herself jerkily and walked up the aisle, her shoes clicking on the hard floor, and she knelt in front of the altar, facing a large cross.

Dober cursed. She was placed so she'd be able to see him and Ivan talking. He hoped she hadn't come for a long praying session. Maybe she'd be gone before Ivan arrived. He watched her as she turned her face up to one of the statues, and his mind drifted guiltily back to Stefan. This church was where people took their guilt and regrets, but he found no comfort here. Comfort came in the sense of doing his duty, a good professional job, outwitting the other side. This was the front line; Stefan was a war casualty just as much as if he'd fallen in battle. People back home didn't realize that.

Watching the girl praying—her lips were moving like a semiliterate person reading—he remembered telling Stefan that Catholicism in Poland reminded him of a hardy weed that refused to be uprooted. Stefan himself still wore a St. Christopher medal round his neck, not for religious reasons, but because his dead mother had given it to him. "Frank," Stefan had told him, "you'll never understand the Poles. You'd have to be born here. . . ."

At that moment he saw Ivan enter silently and glance around: at the old women and at the girl still praying intensely—for what?—at the altar. He was thirty-three, handsome in a bold, big-boned way, and elegant, dressed this time in a long black leather coat and high boots. He liked clothes and women—that was how they had recruited him: by offering him the means to buy both. He was always in need of money apparently. He was having an affair with an extravagant Polish woman Stefan had introduced him to, a singer in a nightclub Stefan used occasionally for making contacts. They sounded very much in love if you believed the tapes of their conversations in bed. She had fine high cheekbones, a truly beautiful Slavic face, and a strong big-busted body.

21

Ivan had told him once, "When I was young, I only liked women under about a hundred thirty pounds. Now they must be *over* a hundred thirty pounds to satisfy me, with plenty of meat on them . . ." Ivan was his code name. His real name, which was never used, was Leonid Valkonov, and he was one of the cultural attachés at the Soviet embassy. At first Dober hadn't believed their good luck. Contacts in Soviet embassies were extremely rare, and Stefan had had to put the Russian through a long check-up before Dober was satisfied. Although he was the station chief, Headquarters had insisted he deal with Ivan personally.

Ivan summed up the situation in the church very quickly. The old women presented no threat, but the girl had to go before they could talk freely. He walked down the aisle, his boots thudding, and knelt near her. She glanced round at him, uneasy, her concentration gone. In a few minutes she crossed herself abruptly, got up, and walked out.

Ivan didn't hurry. He knelt on as if finishing a prayer. Perhaps he was—perhaps he felt nostalgic for what the crumbling old church represented. It had certainly seemed a strange place to choose for their meeting, but the Russian had insisted. Not many people would be there at that time, he'd said as if he knew it well. It was "very peaceful, very private—*safe*. The last place anybody would look for either of us!"

The old women were preparing to go, buttoning up their heavy coats. They had their backs to the altar, to Ivan, to Dober. After their first inspection, Ivan hadn't interested them any more than the girl. They couldn't have recognized him as a Russian. They were absorbed in their gossip, as if they hadn't met for twenty years; they probably saw each other every day.

Ivan came slowly down the aisle as the old women went out, their voices loud—something scandalous about an abortion. He sat on the bench in front of Dober and grinned back

22

at him, gold teeth flashing arrogantly in the dim light, a faint smell of perfume mingling with the musty smells of the church. Dober had to suppress a feeling of dislike—it wasn't Ivan's fault Stefan had been killed. But no, there was more to it than that. The idea of betraying one's country was repugnant to him—he had to deal with people he frankly, deep down, despised.

"Now we're alone at last. I hope I'm not late. The Poles are holding a mass meeting near the embassy. I had to come another route." Ivan was completely relaxed, unworried, more like an elegant decadent aristocrat of the old Russia than a Soviet bureaucrat. Dober felt unbearably tense behind him—as station chief, he'd got out of practice. "What's the urgency? As if I can't guess."

"We slipped up badly," Dober said.

"We did, too. Moscow's mad about it. The ambassador's been recalled."

"For reassignment?"

"No, for . . . consultation."

"Stefan Michalowski felt very bad about it. He took it as a personal failure."

"We all missed it. It was so beautifully organized."

"And what happens now?"

"It's in the balance."

"Is the Soviet army coming back?"

"We don't know . . . yet."

Dober sat forward anxiously, facing the Russian's handsome profile, and the ancient bench creaked like a rifle shot. "We've got to find out. It's top priority. It's a bad time in Washington—we're in the middle of a very close election campaign and everything becomes more important, especially our mistakes."

"It'll cost you money." The Russian flashed his gold teeth. He always mentioned money as if it were a joke.

"We're prepared to pay, provided we get what we want."

23

He knew from the latest report on Ivan that he'd lost a lot at poker two nights ago. "We've got to know well in advance."

"You knew well in advance about Stefan Michalowski, didn't you?"

Dober whispered impatiently, "A lot of good that did us —or him." But that was unfair. Ivan had risked his own security by telling them. That was one reason he trusted Ivan, and it wasn't the first time Ivan had done it. Also, Stefan had been killed, Ivan said, because the Russians had discovered he worked for the CIA; Ivan now ran the same risk. Dober added more gently, "You were right, but this is much more important."

"Don't worry. The embassy will have to know ahead of time. The ambassador will know when he returns from Moscow. There will also be coded messages."

"When?"

"Meet here on Wednesday."

"Sooner."

"Not possible. I won't know until Wednesday at the earliest."

"Can't you call me?"

"Too risky."

"Leave me a message somewhere safe."

"This is safer." The Russian glanced admiringly round the church. "For me—yes." He rose, lazily stretching. "Been nice talking to you, as you Americans say. Have a good day."

Dober listened to his boots thump down the aisle and over to the door and out. Then he got up and left himself. There was no sign of Ivan outside—no sign of anyone. The street was deserted, silent, extraordinarily peaceful for a country in turmoil.

5

"Are you sure this is the right address?" asked Alec Bruno, staring disapprovingly at the old, rundown apartment building on New York's West Side.

"It's where you asked for," the fat cab driver grunted.

Bruno paid him and got out. In the far distance the sun was going down over New Jersey. Farel had told him on the phone not to get there before five. Farel had sounded no keener on the meeting than he was.

A tall, tanned man in his early fifties who played tennis for an hour every day, Bruno ran the State Department's Soviet desk. He had been a government kremlinologist for over twenty years, and he was against consulting an outsider, even one as distinguished as Farel, but the secretary of state was growing impatient and had vetoed his objections. The CIA's top Soviet source was rumored to be about to deliver, and time was running out if the State Department was going to come up with the answer first. Overseas diplomatic and intelligence reports had produced nothing definite. Warsaw, Berlin, Moscow: all nix. Ditto Bruno's own research and that of his staff. Farel was their last hope for quick results.

Bruno went up to Farel's apartment in a slow, clumsy elevator that seemed to him more suitable for carrying freight than a representative of the State Department. He felt a great sense of letdown—he associated these rundown surroundings more with failure than success. Perhaps he was wasting his time even coming here.

On Farel's floor, the gray walls needed some paint; a dim passage led to a large, ugly door. Worst of all, when Bruno pressed the bell—once, twice, three times—no one answered. Irritated, sure that Farel was deliberately snubbing him— Farel had certainly showed no interest on the phone—Bruno was about to leave when the door suddenly swung open and a girl about twelve looked out. She was plump, with short dark hair, big curious eyes behind moon-shaped glasses, and a firm, determined little chin. She seemed surprised to see Bruno.

"Did you ring?" she asked.

"Several times," Bruno replied, still irritated.

"I'm sorry." Her words came in a rush then. "I was in the john, but I should've heard you. I was just leaving or you'd have been waiting all day." She stared at the bell with disapproval. "We've been having trouble with it. Sometimes it works, sometimes it doesn't." She pressed it with a sudden thrust; there was no sound. "Oh, we'll have to get it fixed. Leo will be very annoyed." She added confidingly, "The trouble is we've got a superintendent who . . . *drinks.*" Her wide brown eyes studied him to see how impressed he was.

"I came to see Mr. Farel," Bruno said impatiently.

At once her manner changed and she became brisk and businesslike. She was at an age when she swung erratically between being childish and being grown-up.

"You must be Mr. Bruno from the State Department. Leo told me you were coming. This way, please." She held the door open. "Leo's still working, Mr. Bruno, but he'll be down any minute now. He just forgets the time when he's onto something."

The apartment matched the building: the rooms were huge and faded, the furniture comfortable but with a slightly battered, much used look. Bruno sat down uneasily on a sagging old couch, the springs groaning under him.

"Would you like a cup of coffee, Mr. Bruno?"

"No, thank you."

"A cup of tea? We've got Chinese and Indian."

Bruno shook his head.

"Have you come from Washington?"

"Yes," he said impatiently. He had no time to waste on children. He had come on very serious State Department business. Where was Farel? "Will your father be long? Perhaps you should tell him I'm here."

"That wouldn't do any good, Mr. Bruno. He locks the door so no one can disturb him. I have orders not even to put a phone call through to him. Sometimes it's very embarrassing. A few weeks ago the White House called and I had to tell them to call back. They were very upset. I've told him I think it's unreasonable. He should make exceptions. But my father doesn't believe in exceptions. He says not making exceptions is the essence of democracy. But I think it's being high-handed."

Bruno heard footsteps in the hallway. A thin, elderly man in a shabby raincoat hesitated when he saw Bruno, then waved to the girl and was gone.

"Goodbye, Henrik," she called after him. "Leo won't be long now," she told Bruno. "Henrik does part-time filing for him. Work must be over for the day." She paused, waiting for Bruno to say something. "Henrik used to be an important statesman in Estonia, where Leo was born." Still no reaction from Bruno (he hadn't come to gossip about ancient Estonians!). "Leo left Estonia in 1940 when the Soviet army took over." She stared desperately round the room in search of a topic. Suddenly she had an inspiration: "Mr. Bruno, do you believe in the transmigration of souls?"

Her challenging look suggested she didn't intend to let Bruno remain silent this time, but he was saved by a quiet voice with a slight foreign accent behind them. "Virgie, Mr.

27

Bruno hasn't come to discuss Hinduism or Buddhism with you, but Poland and the Soviet Union with me."

A small, vigorous man, with thinning black hair and large compelling eyes, came briskly across the room to shake Bruno's hand. The two kremlinologists studied each other carefully with the air of colleagues who are also competitors. Although Bruno had seen Farel in action, most recently at the convention of kremlinologists, he had never met him.

"You must forgive my daughter, Bruno," Farel said jocularly. "She has recently taken up the study of comparative religion and, like all fanatics, she doesn't appreciate that not everyone is as interested as she is."

"Leo, that's not fair."

He patted her dark head affectionately. "I'm doing what you told me to do—telling it like it is."

She looked very serious. "The front doorbell isn't working. Will you tell the super?"

"Virgie, I'd be very grateful if you'd handle it. I'm enormously busy at present. Mr. Bruno and I have a complex problem to solve, and he's come all the way from Washington to work with me on it."

"Okay," she said, not very pleased. "But you know the super pays more attention to you because you've been on television." She had reached the door; she turned her wide brown eyes on each of them in turn. "Don't forget you're meeting me later at the Tagore Restaurant, Leo. Goodbye, Mr. Bruno," and she was gone.

Farel looked apologetically at Bruno. "When we talked on the phone, I forgot this is my daughter's birthday. I always take her out to dinner."

"We haven't much time," Bruno said. "It's extremely urgent. The president must know just as soon as possible."

"We'll lose at the most an hour. We have to eat anyway, Bruno. If you can stand Indian food, maybe you'd like to join us."

28

"I have to get back to Washington."

"You won't have anything to take back tonight."

"You haven't reached any conclusion?" Bruno showed his disappointment.

"No, it still points two ways. I may need several more days."

"Surely not that long."

Farel misread his concern. "Don't worry. We have a guest room—you can stay here if you wish."

Bruno glanced at the sagging couch, the faded lounge. "The State Department usually books me into the Waldorf. I can stay there overnight if it becomes necessary."

"It'll be necessary—unless you want to go back empty-handed."

"You haven't even reached a rough preliminary conclusion?"

"That's not the way I work, Bruno. I conclude nothing until all the evidence is in. No guesses, no leaps in the dark. I'm only halfway through the labor of collecting and sifting all the facts. Somewhere are clues, signs pointing the way. I have yet to find them. You understand the process, Bruno. It'll take time, how much time I can't say."

"It's difficult to appreciate here how very urgent it is. If you were in Washington—"

"If I were in Washington, I'd do no work at all! Everything is a crisis in Washington. It isn't conducive to objective analysis. Too many political interruptions—bad for concentration!"

"Let me tell you how far we've got," Bruno said, hoping to get Farel back to work. Maybe they could cut down the time it would take.

"Let's eat first." Farel was a very precise man who liked to make the reasons clear for all his actions. "Part of my daughter's interest in the transmigration of souls arises from the fact that my wife—her mother—died only a year ago.

29

I've tried to impress on her that afterlives and transmigrations are based on mere speculations with little concrete evidence to support such elaborate structures of belief, but I'm afraid she considers me very cynical—very 'negative.' She's still at the romantic stage when wishful thinking makes you jump to conclusions, usually wrong. That's understandable at twelve, but some kremlinologists go wrong that way, too, and that's inexcusable." He glanced at Bruno to see if he was getting the message. "I want to be of help, Bruno, but not at the expense of my analysis. I also have an obligation to be with my daughter on her birthday. You understand?"

Bruno nodded diplomatically. He didn't want to risk offending Farel until he knew if the famous kremlinologist was on to something.

The restaurant, named after Tagore, had a statue of the bearded Indian sage in the foyer near a tiny cloakroom. The dining room was in the basement, down a winding staircase, dimly lit and smelling strongly of incense. A large carved figure of Krishna stood on a table, and a sitar hung on a wall above a framed quotation from the Bhagavad-Gita.

"There she is," Farel said briskly, peering between the dangling shaded lights, and he set off toward a distant table, where his daughter was sitting with a very tall, slim black youth. "That's one of her friends from school," Farel told Bruno, who began to regret he'd come along.

The youth rose politely to shake hands—he towered over Bruno.

"Willie is a great basketball player, Mr. Bruno," Farel's daughter said. "He's hoping to get a basketball scholarship. He's also a giant."

"I'm not a real giant yet," Willie said. "A giant is officially six feet seven inches. I've got another inch to grow."

"You'll make it, Willie," Farel said.

"I'm not sure I want to, Mr. Farel. I'm big enough now

30

for pro basketball. Every time I grow some more I need something new. I don't even fit the bed no more at my grandmother's."

Farel's daughter impulsively put her arm round him—she could only reach his waist. "I'm proud to know a giant." When a young Indian waiter arrived, she and Willie ordered complicated combinations of Indian dishes. Bruno said he had already eaten. Farel ordered some American food.

"Oh, Leo."

"Virgie, you know I have a weak stomach when I'm working."

"You aren't interested in India. Now if this was the Russian Tea Room . . ."

"You can't be interested in everything. You have to diet intellectually, too."

"You've got a one-track mind, Leo. If a country isn't a fit subject for kremlinology, you're not interested."

"India is not one of the big powers," Bruno began condescendingly, but the child interrupted him. "She may not have lots of nuclear weapons and missiles and oil and money, but India's a big power spiritually, Mr. Bruno. Isn't she, Mr. Gandhi?"

A small, fat Indian manager had arrived to check on the waiter's work, but not for anything was he going to be drawn into an argument between the customers. He said cheerfully, "As our great Rabindranath Tagore, 1861–1941, once wrote, 'When I go from hence let this be my parting word, that what I have seen is unsurpassable.' I hope you may all say that about our cooking." He smiled and departed.

"Farel," Bruno said, "perhaps I could fill you in with a summary of our findings to date."

"Wait," Farel said. "Here comes the food."

Willie stood up, all six feet six inches of him, insisting that they sing "Happy Birthday." Farel beamed at him. They all rose except Virgie, Willie and Farel singing loudly, Bruno merely mouthing the words—this was becoming ridiculous!

Willie produced a present from under his chair—a record album. "You give too much of your time to books," he told her gravely. "Open up. Give music a break." Virgie listened with a serious, upturned face as he talked about the record.

"Farel," Bruno said. "It's getting late."

Farel, who had been watching his daughter with a fond, dreamy look, sat up. "Yes, perhaps this is the right time to creep away." He leaned across the table and said to Willie, "Will you see Virgie home? Mr. Bruno and I must start work."

"I'll have to leave early, too," Willie said apologetically. "I've got a date. I tried to cancel it, but I couldn't get them."

"Here's the money for a cab," Farel said. "That'll save time."

"I'm big enough to see myself home," Virgie said.

"Not on your birthday," her father told her.

When they were outside, Bruno said, "You trust your daughter with that youth?"

Farel seemed surprised. "Willie's been very kind to her since my wife died. His mother died when he was young—it's a bond between them. She goes to watch all his games—it gets her out among people. She went through a brooding period when she didn't want to go out. Even though Willie's three or four years older, he treats her like an equal. That's rare at that age, especially when you're a school basketball star like Willie. He's just a naturally kind fellow. His grandmother comes in to help with the housework and the cooking several days a week. She was a friend of my wife's."

Bruno shrugged. It was none of his business. As they walked past Lincoln Center back to Farel's apartment, he told Farel what they had learned so far—from embassy reports, intelligence findings . . .

"Slim pickings," Farel said thoughtfully, concentrating so completely that he walked into a man crossing the sidewalk

32

in front of them. The man cursed and Farel absentmindedly apologized. "No aerial observation of troop movements? Nothing from the satellites or electronic monitoring?"

"No, nothing."

"You fellows at the State Department still seem to give far too much importance to on-the-spot reports at the expense of objective analysis. Of course you're not as bad as the CIA, who are obsessed with crude front-line spying, but it seems to me your researches too often have the wrong emphasis. I know what I'm talking about, Bruno, because I've made the same mistake myself. Once in Estonia—we lived on the banks of Estonia's largest lake, Peipsi Järve or Lake Peipus —I completely misread the intentions of the Russians. I became too emotionally involved. I didn't want to leave Estonia and go into a life of exile. I wanted to stay by Lake Peipus with my parents forever. It was unbelievably beautiful in those days, though it's probably lined with Soviet factories now! So through wishful thinking, my analysis was completely wrong and we barely made it across the border before the Soviet army took over. Never again! Agents on the spot sometimes make the same error."

The elevator had taken them up while he had been talking, and he had opened the apartment door.

"Now I'll show you where I work."

He led Bruno down the hallway to the stairs. At the top was an ivory-colored door. Farel laughed as he unlocked it. "Virgie painted this. She thought an ivory tower ought to have an ivory door." Beyond was an immense room as tidy, abstract, and methodical in appearance as the rest of the apartment was messily human and lived in. There were neat floor-to-ceiling bookshelves arranged alphabetically, carefully stacked mountains of foreign newspapers and magazines and reports of all kinds in European and Asian languages, rows of machines for copying and recording and receiving agency news reports, and—completely lining two

33

of the walls—what Farel called "the heart of the matter": his filing cabinets containing the data of thirty years.

"The lonely life has its advantages, Bruno. When one does all one's own research, one can combine it all in one's mind and reach conclusions immediately, unlike staff or team work, when you need to put all your heads together and pool what you've got to make the right connections. Apart from a part-time file clerk, I run a one-man operation."

"I'm surprised you don't use computers more."

"They have their limitations—and their dangers. In my opinion, they're best used to sift and assemble the evidence once you know what facts you're looking for. You know yourself, Bruno, how easy the clues are to miss. A slight divergence from past Soviet pronouncements, a shift in emphasis in Chinese statements, a hint between the lines of some obscure journal. For that work, you need the best computer of all—the human computer!"

"With all its human weaknesses."

"But reduced in my case to their minimum—one person. In the State Department, and above all in the CIA, you have a human chain with weaknesses in every link!"

Bruno kept his disagreement to himself. He was a great believer in computers. But it was natural, he told himself, that, without all the expensive technological aids and foreign staff he at the State Department could call upon, an independent like Farel should try to minimize their importance. Looking at the old-fashioned and comparatively skimpy equipment of Farel's study, Bruno had to keep reminding himself that it was here that some uniquely successful analyses and predictions had been made.

"How did you get on to the Polish uprising?" he asked. "Everybody else missed it."

Farel grinned boyishly. "You really want to know? It was really a reward for being well read. I'm not as choosey as you at the State Department and the CIA sometimes are. My

34

reading doesn't have to have status or official significance. I'm willing to read anything within the sphere of my study. Nothing's beneath my attention, not even the graffiti of Moscow toilets! I sometimes read for as long as twelve or even fifteen hours a day. You can get through a lot of literature that way. I found myself studying the social activities at the Polish factories because there was more and more coverage in newspapers and journals. I couldn't help noticing there were suddenly many more reports of fraternizing between factories—more inter-factory sports, more inter-factory social events. I went back to my files on the worker demonstrations of 1956 and 1970, and I noticed the same sudden increase in contacts between workers at different factories. With my mind pointed in that direction, I assembled more and more evidence that something was happening among the workers similar to 1956 and 1970 until the evidence was overwhelming and the conclusion inevitable. In fact, those inter-factory social events were how they organized the uprising on a national level—it enabled them to travel and meet without suspicion."

"Our ambassador was invited to present the trophies at one factory," Bruno said bitterly. "How did we come to miss it at the time?"

"Like the Russians, maybe you missed the wood for the trees. It wasn't what you were looking for."

The room had huge windows covered by heavy dark curtains. As if aware the subject of his success was painful to Bruno, Farel pulled back the curtains, telling him, "Here's a fine view of Central Park." Bruno caught a glimpse of lights twinkling in an expanse of warm darkness beneath a beautiful clear sky. The curtains were quickly drawn again. "Too distracting," Farel said. "For artists, not kremlinologists."

He sat down on a straight-backed wooden chair and passed a hand over his eyes.

"I'm sorry, Bruno. I'm a creature of habit. This is my

35

usual bedtime. My body switches off like a machine."

"We ought to push on," Bruno said, his tennis player's body still up on his heavy daily dose of vitamins. "Are you on to something?"

"There is something . . ." Farel's voice was low, hard to hear. "But it's too early to tell for sure . . ."

"What is it?" Bruno asked casually, pretending to scan Farel's bookshelves. If he sounded too eager, he might make Farel even more cautious. "What have you found?"

No reply.

The famous kremlinologist was asleep, his mouth slightly open, as calm and untroubled as a baby.

6

Ursula Rogal hurried home. She wanted to catch the seven
o'clock news. The media, short of foreign dramas, were playing up the Polish situation, and maybe tonight they would
have the answer to what the Russians were going to do. She
was worried about her relatives in Warsaw. She had tried to
phone them the night before, but she couldn't get through.
All the lines were busy; the overseas operator told her there
was an indefinite wait. Maybe she'd try again tonight—after
he left . . .

One of the boys in the supermarket waved to her—not one
she recognized, though the wave and the grin were familiar,
knowing. The grave Chinese in the laundry inclined his head
as she passed. That was quite a tribute coming from him—
usually he was as impassive as the small statue of Buddha he
had on his counter. She was respected here—Miss Rogal the
schoolteacher, so dedicated to her work that she even had
students come to her home for extra lessons. Nobody guessed
her secret.

"Someone's been to see you." Tony, the old super, was
fussing over the garbage bags outside the building. That was
all Tony did—that and gossip. "You just missed 'em." His
eyes went over her breasts, the old devil, as she collected her
mail from the box—the telephone bill and a newspaper from
Poland.

37

"Who was it?"

"Didn't see 'em. I was in the back. Mrs. Charles told me you had a visitor."

Mrs. Charles was the crazy old widow in the next-door apartment who talked to her plants and was always complaining, her nose into everything. To hell with her. Nobody was waiting at the top of the stairs. Maybe whoever it was would come back.

"Miss Rogal!"

Mrs. Charles had opened her door. She must have been waiting, the old peeping Tom.

"You missed one of your young men." She had a baggy flowered dress on and her hair in curlers; she looked a mess. Old age was no excuse.

"What did he look like?"

"That very tall black one." The old woman looked at her. "He's a man, not a boy. You have to teach them that big?"

"They come in all sizes."

She'd told him to come at eight. Why had he come so early?

As she let herself into her apartment, her body felt worn down. Maybe it was the cocktails she'd had with Fran, or maybe she was overdoing it and she ought to take it easy, not see any of them for a few days. She was within spitting distance of forty-five—her birthday was only ten days off. That wasn't old, but it certainly wasn't young either. In five years she'd be fifty—half a century! Already she had to touch up her hair and use lots more make-up, and she didn't like anybody to see her when she first woke up, especially around the eyes. That was why she never let anybody stay all night. But she still kept her figure—she would have made a great model. She always kept to her Weight-Watcher's diet. That way you stayed young as long as possible, that and being active.

She switched on the TV—the news was just coming on.

38

The files she'd borrowed from Fran were spread over the couch, and she put them on the table so she could sit down. The file on Auschwitz was on top. It had told her all she wanted to know. After the news, she'd get out the uniform ready for him.

She picked up the newspaper from Poland . . . and her bell buzzed.

He'd come back already. What was his problem?

She peered through the peephole, hesitated, then opened the door.

"Hello," he said as if unsure of his reception.

"Why have you come now? All right, come in. I'm just watching the news."

She sat on the couch; he sat beside her, stretching out his legs. The first news item concerned the president. He'd been campaigning in New York, and there were quick glimpses of him waving and grinning in the garment district. Someone asked him about unemployment, Federal aid for the city—why didn't they ask him about Poland?

"Why did you come?" she said.

"Are you really going to tell?"

"I might," she said, facing him.

"You mustn't."

"It's up to you."

"It'll ruin everything . . . my life . . ."

In his high emotional state, he leaned toward her, grasping her shoulder. She felt the strength of his fingers, the hard tension. But she ignored the warning.

"Don't touch me."

"Promise me you won't."

"I told you, it's up to you."

His grip tightened.

"You're hurting me."

He had gotten the wrong idea: she didn't want to play any games now. Wait until later, when he put on the uniform.

She was too age-conscious to wear glasses and she only really noticed the expression in his eyes when he moved closer. She'd badly misread his reaction. He was really worked up, on edge. She better backpedal and calm him down.

"Now stop it. Let's talk about it."

His hand moved up to her throat.

"Take your hand awa—"

He squeezed, silencing her.

She panicked then and began to struggle wildly. He was really strong—and determined. She felt his urgency, his impatience. Her mind raced for help . . . the old woman next door! Too old! . . . But if she could only fight him off long enough to scream, that might scare him away. She tried to speak, tried to tell him, *All right, I promise. I promise!* But it was too late. Both his hands were on her throat now while the rest of his body held her down, and slowly the life was squeezed out of her—painfully, chokingly. Her mind flashed back to Poland—this was the end of all that had begun there —and a red mist clouding her head changed abruptly into darkness. Her legs twitched once or twice, a reflex action, and then her body was lifeless. Slowly his hands relaxed.

He listened, but the house was quiet. Nobody had heard their struggle.

He slowly sat back, looking at his hands. His rage had spent itself and now fear was flooding in, but he still had something else to do before he left, and he couldn't afford to take long.

The TV news was just reaching Poland. There was a glimpse of street demonstrations, the outside of the Soviet embassy, a statement from a nervous government spokesman —no news yet. But in any case she was beyond worrying about her relatives in Warsaw now, and he wasn't interested. He left the TV on merely as a covering noise while he rapidly searched the apartment. It was soon found. . . .

*   *   *

40

A short time later, the bell buzzed again.

A short, stocky middle-aged Catholic priest was at the door. In his neat clerical black suit, holding a briefcase, he might easily have been mistaken for a businessman.

No one answered his ring.

He could hear voices inside the apartment. He pressed the bell again and then knocked. Mrs. Charles, her hair still in curlers, came out of her apartment.

"She's in there. I heard her let someone in not too long ago —one of her students."

"I can hear voices," the priest said.

"Perhaps she didn't hear you. Let me try." Mrs. Charles pressed down hard and kept her finger on the bell for several moments, then pressed it again and again. "That'd wake the dead." She smiled knowingly at the priest. "Maybe she doesn't want to be disturbed."

"She's expecting me. She asked me to come. We made an appointment"—he glanced at his wristwatch—"for seven-thirty. I'm a few minutes early."

The old super came up the stairs. He seemed surprised to see the priest. "Not got in yet, Father?"

"I was just leaving, but this lady said Miss Rogal was definitely in. And I can hear voices . . ."

"Try it again." The old super pressed this time—several times—and listened. "That's not her, it's her TV. 'Family Crisis' follows the news. Maybe she doesn't want any visitors."

"That's what I said," Mrs. Charles told him.

"No, no, I have an appointment." The priest seemed irritated. "Perhaps she's visiting one of the neighbors."

"The only one she socializes with is Mr. Rivera upstairs." The old super knew all the tenants' habits. "I'll check if she's there." He went laboriously up the stairs. They heard a knock and then voices, and he came down again accompanied by a slim, dark-haired man who was dressed for going

41

out. "This is Mr. Rivera," the old super said to the priest. "He hasn't seen her."

"I hope nothing's wrong," the priest said nervously.

Rivera pressed the bell and listened.

"She may have gone out again when I was in the back," the old super said.

"No, no, she was expecting me," the priest said. "She called me earlier, and we made an appointment."

"Haven't you got a key, Tony?" Rivera said impatiently.

"Tenants don't like it," the old super said. He took out a large, crowded key ring. "But Miss Rogal, she's an understanding lady. Will you back me up?"

"Sure," Rivera said. "The worst that can happen is that you'll find her in bed with some dude."

"Perhaps I should leave," the priest said, "And come back later."

"Something could have happened," the old super said. "Had a tenant once who had a heart attack in the bath. Water ran under the door."

"Go ahead, man," Rivera said.

The old super found the right key and unlocked the door and pushed it half open. "Miss Rogal," he called in a low voice, as if expecting to be bawled out. Then he went in. "Good God," he murmured when he saw the ransacked apartment. And then he noticed the crumpled body on the couch . . .

The precinct's homicide record was bad. Homicides were well up on last year, while the rate of solved cases was the lowest of any precinct in Manhattan. Detective Sergeant Carl Snyder, a gruff, canny veteran of eighteen years with the New York Police Department, felt under great pressure to come up with a quick solution as he examined Ursula Rogal's ransacked room and questioned the people who had found the body. Bodies were seldom found so quickly—that was an advantage anyway. And the witnesses were still in a shocked, confused state and might let slip something revealing.

Tony Ronsowski, the old superintendent, came first. Snyder knew his type well, an old semiliterate immigrant from eastern Europe with a built-in fear of the police, a natural informer on any block. Shock—and some liquor—had loosened his tongue and Snyder, for all his experience, had difficulty in keeping him to the point: how long he had been out front after Ursula Rogal had gone in and who else had he seen enter the building after her.

The priest and Rivera had gone in after her, nobody else.

"Were you outside the whole time until you went upstairs and discovered the body?"

The old super was silent a moment, thinking. "I went to the john once."

"How long were you gone?"

The old super hesitated.

Snyder said impatiently, "I'm not asking you what you did in the john, only how long you were gone."

"About five minutes. Long enough to pee."

"And long enough for someone to go in without being seen. Did you go inside for anything else?"

"To feed my dog."

"How long did that take?"

"The food was ready. Long enough to dish it out, that's all. I came right back out again. I was tying up the garbage bags."

About all Snyder established was that someone could have got in—and out—without being seen. But their timing would have had to be pretty good. Strangulations, in his experience, were impulsive, not premeditated; that meant the killer would have to improvise in getting away, and that was when you made your mistakes.

Vera Charles was the kind of old nosy neighbor it was easy

43

not to take seriously, but sometimes they were more useful as informers than the supers. She had been the last person to speak to the dead woman—except for the killer. She had heard the killer arrive. "I was watching the seven o'clock news, and I heard her open her door and then his voice. He'd been there earlier before she got home. A big hulking brute of a boy. I'd be scared to try to teach someone like that. She was so nice she even gave them lessons at her home. And that's what you get for it—robbed and murdered!"

Snyder tried to hide his excitement. "Are you sure it was this student of hers? You didn't see him—"

"Oh, I didn't need to. I recognized his heavy step and his deep voice. I turned down the news to listen . . ."

It was what he'd been looking for. A point had been established and his mind turned in a certain direction.

Father Brian Joyce, a short, stocky man with a pink complexion and thick, graying hair, was the kind of easygoing Irish-American often found in the priesthood—or the police. Snyder felt at ease with him at once. You could talk realistically with this kind of priest, even joke with him; you didn't have to be careful with your questions.

"Were you a friend of Miss Rogal's, Father?" he asked as soon as they faced each other.

The priest shook his head. "I hardly knew her, Mr. Snyder. She phoned us a couple of weeks ago. Before then, I didn't know the lady existed. She'd been born a Catholic—in Poland. She gave up attending church in her teens apparently, but she'd recently decided she wanted to come back to the Church. But first she wanted to take a course of religious instruction—a refresher course. I met her for about half an hour, decided she was quite sincere about it, and arranged to visit her at seven-thirty this evening to begin her instruction. She died before she could return to the Church. It's tragic. But the wish was there, the grace . . ."

"Do you usually come to people's homes, Father, or do

they generally come to you for instruction?"

"Either way, Mr. Snyder. But I believe in the value of home visiting, seeing people in their own environment, particularly in the case of lapsed Catholics. Miss Rogal seemed rather shy and nervous. I didn't want her to change her mind on that account, so I tried to make it as easy as possible for her. At first when I couldn't get any answer—I was a little early—I thought she must have decided against it and didn't want to face me. But then I heard voices, so I supposed she'd had an unexpected visitor—she told me she gave extra lessons at home. But sometimes you lose people that way, by going away. Sometimes they never call you back. They're always meaning to make another appointment but never do, so I went back and pressed her doorbell again. The rest, I think, you know, Mr. Snyder."

"Did you see anybody when you were coming in or while you were waiting?"

"Only the superintendent. Then, of course, later Mrs. Charles came out of her apartment. You know what happened from then on."

"Why do you think she wanted to rejoin your church after all these years—in her forties?"

"It's an age at which people sometimes do some thinking. She said she found life empty on her own. It's a state of mind well known to theologians, Mr. Snyder—the brink of despair."

"Was she depressed about anything?"

"She was worried about her relatives in Poland during the present troubles, but I was speaking of a spiritual state, Mr. Snyder."

That was the first time the priest had tried to pull rank on him. Snyder said bluntly, "She didn't say anything that might explain why someone would want to murder her?"

"No. She seemed a very normal, kindly woman, as far as I could tell—a very good, conscientious teacher, I'm sure."

45

"Did she mention any of her students?"

Father Joyce replied slowly, thoughtfully, "No, she didn't say anything about any particular student, nothing specific. She mentioned the overcrowding in public schools—she had forty-one students in one of her classes. It's not unheard of, we all know, for a teacher to be assaulted by the older boys. Of course they're not boys at that age, they're men, at least physically, with a lot of frustrated energy they don't know what to do with. Often they've had little or no religious training and have no moral sense. I think she made a mistake giving extra teaching at home. I told her so."

"What did she say?"

"She laughed. But how much did she really know about her students? She was inviting strangers into her home."

"The killer wasn't a stranger," Snyder said impatiently. He hadn't time to listen to moralizing. Every second counted now—he was on to something. "Thanks, Father, for your help."

The priest seemed relieved and suddenly tired, older. Finding the body had obviously been a shock to him, Snyder thought. It was sometimes hard for an experienced cop to remember how ordinary people reacted to murder.

Next came Al Rivera, a slim dark-haired man in his thirties, born in Puerto Rico but a New Yorker since his teens. He was a masseur at an athletic club and was poised and calm throughout the police questioning. You would have thought he discovered dead bodies every day. He must have feared he wasn't making a good impression, because he mentioned his combat service with the army in Vietnam—"I got used to seeing people who'd been killed. One river had so many dead bodies it was like beef stew." He had a neat, fussed-over appearance, even to polished fingernails, but his bearing was aggressive, macho. This sense of conflict in him opened up Snyder's own prejudices; he typed Rivera as probably bisexual.

46

"You and Miss Rogal were close friends?"

"Hell, no." Flash of perfect white teeth. "She wasn't my type. Too old. We were just neighbors. Sometimes had a cup of coffee together, a gossip. That's all."

"You ever meet any of her students?"

"I sometimes passed one of them on the stairs. A very big guy—black. Made me feel like a midget. I asked her about him, but she didn't want to talk about him. I got the idea she was worried about him. A dumb ox maybe, with low grades. But I didn't ask her. It was her own business."

Snyder didn't probe any deeper. Why waste time on Rivera now? He could always come back to him. He had what he wanted, a suspect. Now he had to find him.

7

The Soviet ambassador had extended his stay in Moscow, and so Ivan had postponed their meeting for two days. Washington had taken the news very badly—they were counting on Ivan!—but there was nothing Dober could do about it.

An American optimist by upbringing, Dober had learned to be a fatalist since coming to Eastern Europe. The Communist countries had a different rhythm! Washington, with the rhythm of back home, came on as if he had the power to get faster results if he'd only get up off his ass. The idea of being so dependent on Ivan—a Russian—was repugnant to them. "Promise him a bonus—anything," Washington had said as if money would solve everything.

He'd already given Ivan fifteen thousand bucks—Ivan always wanted to be paid in dollars, never Polish currency—and there was another fifteen thousand when he came through. Thirty thousand bucks, even under inflation, wasn't chicken feed for just one piece of information, and on top of that there was Ivan's fat retainer. The shrewd Russian didn't come cheap, but more money wouldn't persuade him to take any more risks than he was already taking. Ivan had to protect himself. Even when he knew what was going to happen, he'd tell only when he thought it was safe. Washington would have to play a waiting game a little longer, Dober

48

thought. Like him. Only they didn't have to watch Poland slowly falling apart.

Along some of the streets now, you had to leave your car and walk. Barricades were going up as if the workers knew the news ahead of Ivan and were expecting the Russians at any minute. Militant leaders went from district to district addressing mass rallies. Only some of the older workers kept silent, remembering the hopelessness of their opposition to Soviet tanks a few years ago. How philosophical the barricades would have made Stefan about Polish pride! Dober missed the Polish journalist's insights into Polish character. The other Polish agents turned in only routine factual reports.

Dober attended an embassy political meeting at which the ambassador, an old army man, ridiculed the workers: he talked as if their "foolishness" might cause a world war. He reminded Dober of something Stefan had once said: "Our pride is our paradox, keeping us alive as a nation but also risking our life." The ambassador saw only the risk; of course he was concerned, too, for the safety of the embassy in the case of a Soviet attack. He asked Dober if he had any news. They all looked to the CIA for the answer to what the Russians were going to do.

At an embassy cocktail party for a visiting American orchestra, he met Ivan, who was very cool and distant, but later while he was chatting with the French ambassador, Dober noticed Ivan walk over to his wife, and soon she was laughing at something the handsome young Russian told her. On the way home, he asked her what Ivan had talked about. "He asked me if I was married, and when I said yes, he asked what my husband did. I said you worked at the embassy. He said all Americans in Poland claimed to work at the embassy. He asked what your real job was. I just laughed . . ." Ivan was certainly a cool one.

The Agency instructed him to move his family to Berlin

in case of a Soviet invasion. He didn't want to be separated from them—he didn't like the idea of his wife alone in Berlin —but he had to agree it would leave him freer to operate if he ran into trouble over Ivan. Mills in Berlin, who was married and therefore no threat presumably, would take care of them until it was safe for them to return . . . or he joined them.

Moving children involved so many things. It was probably easier moving an army. They were so busy the last day packing, checking, finding this, arranging that, getting the kids ready, that he and his wife had no time for a final talk. She kissed him several times and held onto him, which was unlike her because she wasn't a demonstrative woman in public, and a lot of people were watching, including the usual Soviet shadows (they didn't matter here, but he always had to lose them before he met Ivan). He watched the plane take off, with a grim feeling he might never see his family again. Maybe his wife had felt the same way—she sometimes caught her mood from him. It was the effect of the difference in their ages. The only consolation was that he'd felt this way at other times when he and his wife were separated. And they were still together.

The apartment was as lonely as a bachelor's; he attended a reception at the embassy just to get away. Since Washington had told him to handle Ivan personally, he'd used that as an excuse to neglect the social side of the station chief's work, but now he was content to waste time chatting with the usual cross section of embassy and Polish people. These receptions had been one of Stefan's hunting grounds; it was there Stefan had first met Ivan. Now the conversation was almost wholly about "the situation" and what was going to happen, and everyone left early. Back home, he tried to do some reading in Polish history, taking book after book down from the shelves, but he was unable to concentrate for long.

He was as impatient as Washington now for his next meeting with Ivan.

It had been a trying day. Reason and logic had led him down several long blind alleys, and the cry of satisfaction that usually announced he was at last on the right track had yet to come. It was not to come that afternoon. One moment the whole apartment had a perfect stillness ideal for working in; the next moment the stillness, the silence, the peace had been completely shattered and his concentration ruined.

The front door banged open.

The front door slammed shut.

There was a hurried dash across the lounge and frantic feet on the stairs.

Farel, who claimed he could hear a TV or radio played at minimum volume on the floor below, registered all these sounds with the sensitiveness of a seismograph, noting that the noise steadily increased in volume until there was a series of thunderous knocks at the door of the Ivory Tower itself.

Such a disturbance of his working hours had never happened before; it could mean only a great emergency. The day had begun badly, and his futile attempts to find the right track in his reasoning had obviously been a preparation for an even worse disaster. He unlocked the door with the same kind of distraught expression that Beethoven might have had if he'd been disturbed during the composition of the "Choral" Symphony. "What the devil's happened?" he asked. "Is the building on fire?"

"Oh, Leo!" Virgie cried and burst into tears.

Farel had seen his young daughter cry so seldom—in fact, the only other time he could remember was at his wife's funeral—that this had a powerful effect on him and confirmed his impression that a great disaster must have struck New York. His first thought was for his files, the

51

irreplaceable accumulation of thirty years.

"Virgie," he said urgently, trying to speak calmly, "you must tell me what has happened."

She couldn't get it out. He took her by the arms and shook her gently. Her tears slowed to a stop, but she was still incoherent. Was this the daughter he'd taught to be articulate at all times, never blinded by emotion? He felt impatient with her and tried to control himself. Yet there might be little time left in which to act, to save their lives—and the files.

He led her down to the floor below—she might be calmer sitting down. No sign of smoke was in the apartment—yet; perhaps it already filled the elevator shaft outside and would at any moment come seeping under the front door. Virgie had probably come upstairs at the risk of her own life to warn him. He said quietly, "Now tell me all about it, Virgie."

She looked at him with big, tearful eyes—never had she seemed more like her mother! His calm, unflurried appearance on the surface (he was churning and boiling inside) calmed her slowly. The moan of a stricken animal trailed away and she won back control of her voice.

"Leo," she said in a broken, little-girl tone punctuated by the occasional sob, "a woman's been murdered and, oh, they've arrested Willie!" Tears began to trickle again.

"What?" Farel was stunned. Relief about his files changed to impatience; all the churning and boiling inside shot to the surface and he glowered down at his daughter. "Virgie, have you completely destroyed my concentration just to tell me— *this?*"

The tears began to flow more quickly and she moaned up at him, "Leo, you don't understand. The police have arrested Willie—for *murder!*"

"I understand very well!" he shouted back at her. All the frustrations of a bad day were coming out now. He walked angrily up and down in front of her. "I understand that you have interrupted my work, ruined hours of analysis, just to tell me about this sordid, trivial matter! We could just as well have discussed it when I finished work. You have broken your agreement never to disturb me except in the case of a grave emergency!"

"This is a grave emergency. I thought you'd be able to help him."

"Help him? If he's been foolish enough to go around murdering people, he'll have to pay for it."

"But he's innocent, I know he is. The police've got to find somebody, so they've picked on Willie."

"How do you know he's innocent? You know him on a social level. He's been kind to you, but otherwise you don't know much about him. The police are not altogether stupid, Virgie, whatever you may see on television. They wouldn't arrest him unless they had a reasonable case against him."

"They have arrested innocent people before."

"The percentage of innocent people arrested is probably very low."

"How do you know, Leo? It's not like you to deal in *probably*s."

"And it's not like you, Virgie, to behave like a hysterical, foolish little girl, overcome by female emotionalism. I thought our lives were in great danger when you took it upon yourself to interrupt—no, to disrupt—my work! I'm sorry about what has happened to your friend Willie, but there is absolutely nothing I can do about it." He strode back to the stairs. "I trust this will never happen again short of a nuclear raid or the apocalypse!" And he went angrily up the stairs, entered the Ivory Tower, and slammed the door behind him in case she was in any doubt as to how he felt. She wasn't.

He feared that the violent interruption would have made his work impossible for the rest of the day, but no sooner had he restudied the problem and gone over his false starts than he suddenly found his first real clue as to Soviet intentions, and all the connections that had been eluding him became clear. His work was off on the right track at last, off and running. It went so well that within an hour, when his first clue was confirmed by several others, he was on his way to a conclusion, and all that remained to be done was to find the rest of the supporting evidence, which he knew was somewhere close at hand, if not exactly where, in his line of filing cabinets. Finding it was a routine, time-consuming chore he could safely leave until the next morning when Henrik would be there to help him.

He sat back with a pleased sense of achievement, his good humor completely restored, and his mind, now free of analysing the labyrinthine motives and actions of the Soviet Union, inevitably went back to Virgie, but this time more sympathetically. The child had been very upset. Perhaps he should have been a little more understanding and, once disturbed and taken away from his work, have given her more of his time. Well, she would be calmer and more reasonable now and they could talk it over much more rationally.

No sooner decided than done. Farel went downstairs, cheerfully humming an old Estonian folk song of his youth. There was no sign of Virgie in the living room. She wasn't in the kitchen. Perhaps she had gone outside to seek comfort elsewhere. He glanced in her room and there she was, lying on the bed reading a diet book.

"Virgie."

No answer, head still deep in book.

"Virgie, I'd like to talk to you."

She looked up without speaking, her expression serious and cold. Her eyes were red-rimmed and bloodshot, but she was perfectly composed, as poised as she usually was—but colder.

He sat on the edge of the bed. She didn't move.

"I didn't know, Virgie, that Willie meant so much to you . . ." No, that was the wrong way to get into it, he could tell

54

that by her face. "Your concern is admirable. Human, involved, loyal. No man is an island . . . But you must also
understand that the American police do not arrest someone
unless they have convincing evidence against him." She
stared coldly at him. The situation was ridiculous. He'd
come to forgive her for all the trouble she'd caused, but here
she was treating him as if he were the one in the wrong.
"Who was the woman Willie is suspected of killing?"

"His schoolteacher."

He had a sudden vision of a classroom flare-up, of six
feet–six inch Willie losing his temper. These American
schools had no real discipline! In Estonia, when he was a boy,
a schoolteacher was God . . .

"If it took place at school, there must be many witnesses—"

"She was found murdered in her apartment."

"Why then is Willie suspected?"

"He used to go there for extra teaching. Oh, but he didn't
do it!"

"The police must know something you don't, Virgie.
They're trained for that kind of work."

She said indignantly, "You taught me to question everything. If you took that attitude in your work, you'd swallow
everything the Soviet and Chinese governments say."

"But the New York City Police Department isn't comparable to the governments of nearly a thousand million people,
nor is an individual murder case with one victim and a single
person accused comparable to a problem involving whole
nations."

"I don't see the difference," she said. "It's only a matter
of numbers."

"It's a matter of degree. Adequately trained police are
competent to deal with a simple murder mystery, whereas
you need highly developed powers of analysis to solve the

55

mysteries of nations—a special ability akin to a marriage between a scientist and an artist. A kremlinologist at his peak is their offspring!"

Virgie wasn't impressed. "All the more reason, Leo, why I thought you'd be able to help Willie."

"Virgie, I'm willing to do everything within reason. If he hasn't got a good lawyer, we'll get him one. Willie seems a nice fellow, not the kind to go round murdering schoolteachers, whatever he held against them, but you must admit we really know very little about him."

"We know enough. Willie is my friend. I know if you looked into it the way you look into Soviet affairs, he'd soon be free."

"What is it the Americans say? You don't need a steam-hammer to crack a nut. My dear Virgie, I haven't the time to devote to the single problems of individuals. The police have logical powers of an ABC nature—more than enough for their work—and they have all the manpower and time they need. But I'm only one man. I never have enough time for all the subtleties and complexities of my own work, which is XYZ in comparison. And at the present time I have had to drop everything to concentrate on this appeal for assistance from the State Department. I have just obtained the first important clue."

She wasn't interested. "You could spare five minutes for Willie."

"Five minutes? I'm not a miracle worker." He felt annoyed and frustrated. "Virgie, you're being very unreasonable. Think about what I've just said, and we'll discuss it over dinner."

He went back to the Ivory Tower. There was more satisfaction in a routine search for evidence in the files than arguing pointlessly with her. Virgie was as obstinate as her mother—obstinacy was a famous Estonian trait, although her mother had been American, of Irish ancestry, from the state of Maine.

He had arranged to meet Bruno in the evening to go over the day's progress, but Bruno, impatient for news, phoned from the Waldorf, and Farel told him to come right over. He needed somebody to talk to who understood the importance of what he'd done.

Bruno arrived with a loaded briefcase. "I've had all the latest diplomatic and intelligence reports flown over from Washington."

Farel quickly went through them. "Nothing here. Didn't the satellites produce anything? Or radio reconnaissance along the Polish border?"

"Nothing."

"Perhaps Soviet camouflage is too clever."

Bruno asked grumpily, "Did you make any progress?"

"As a matter of fact," Farel said, growing more cheerful, "I think I've got it—a really significant clue that unmasks their real intentions at last."

"You sure?" Bruno was as excited as Farel. "Which way does it point—back in or stay out?"

"Let me show you. Here, sit at my desk so I can spread the evidence out in front of you." Farel was suddenly as enthusiastic as a boy. He went to one of the filing cabinets and took out a small, badly printed newspaper. "Before I show you this," he said, "I must make one condition. You mustn't tell Washington until I'm fully satisfied. It'll probably take another twenty-four hours."

"Very well."

Farel opened the newspaper to an inside page where he had ringed a paragraph in red. "I obtained this obscure publication from an old Estonian friend. You see what this paragraph says? Soldier's marriage postponed because his leave has been cancelled! Brood on that, Bruno." He went

57

back to the filing cabinet and took out a cheap magazine. He opened it at the sports section, where he had circled a paragraph at the bottom of a page. He laid it in front of Bruno. "You see? Football match between an army unit and a local team has been cancelled. Very well. You see the trend, Bruno?" Bruno nodded; he looked grave. "I've found five other examples of army leaves being cancelled, events involving the army being postponed, all in very obscure local publications—so obscure and local that Soviet censorship might easily miss them or think them safely out of range of even the sharpest eyes of Western kremlinology. You see, Bruno, the classical humdrum methods still pay even in the age of technology!"

"Your conclusion then," Bruno said gravely, "is that the Soviet army is going back in?"

"It all points to that, but 'all' so far consists of only a few examples. We need more before we can be sure. My assistant and I will spend the whole of tomorrow combing all possible places."

"I should warn the secretary of state immediately. The president must be told. God knows what he'll do. The latest poll shows him two points behind."

"All the more reason why we must be sure. Remember your promise, Bruno. If the rest of the evidence is positive, we should be ready to release it by tomorrow night."

"Can't you do it any quicker? Perhaps you could work through the night. I'll assist you."

"You aren't familiar with my methods or my files here. You must let me do it my own way, Bruno. Once I'm satisfied, then you can take over, but not until then . . ."

The two men went down to dinner, Farel relaxed and cheerful, Bruno tense and impatient.

Sitting with Virgie was a middle-aged black woman, small but formidable. Virgie introduced her to Bruno as Willie's grandmother.

"They won't even let Mrs. Lee see him," Virgie told her father.

"That's right, Mr. Farel," Willie's grandmother said.

The two of them had obviously formed an alliance. Farel's cheerfulness ebbed away.

"Mrs. Lee," he said sympathetically, "I was sorry to hear the news. Has Willie got a good lawyer?"

"Leo," Virgie said severely, "didn't you hear me say they wouldn't even let her see him?"

"Beating him up," Willie's grandmother said.

"What's happened?" Bruno asked. They were wasting Farel's time; he had to get him back to work.

"You met Willie. He's been arrested for murder."

"They're beating a confession out of him. Mr. Farel, you must stop them. Virgie says you're real smart at finding out the truth about the Russians."

"Leo," Virgie said, "you've often claimed your methods are applicable to any human situation, great or small. Here's your chance to prove it."

Farel felt himself being cornered. He couldn't meet the grandmother's eyes. "But I'm not a policeman, Virgie! To ask a highly experienced international analyst like myself to devote time to a simple murder case is like asking Einstein to add up a grocery bill. I'll get Willie a good criminal lawyer. He'll take care of it."

"Exactly." Bruno was irritated by the ridiculous argument. My God, didn't they realize Farel was working on a matter of grave international importance! "A competent criminal lawyer is what you need. Mr. Farel has to complete an analysis for the president."

"They're beating him up," Willie's grandmother said as if Bruno hadn't spoken. "Mr. Farel, you've got to stop them."

The grandmother and his daughter both stared at him.

He knew when he was beaten.

"Very well," Farel said irritably. "While the fate of Poland

59

hangs in the balance and I may be the only one in the outside world who is on to what the Soviet Union intends to do, I'll go and try to see Willie. Nobody seems to care a damn about my work!"

He went to the closet to get his topcoat.

8

Bruno made a call to Washington and Washington called the police commissioner, with the result that Farel was received very respectfully at the police precinct. There was a short delay, however, before he could see Willie. Willie had been undergoing a rough, intensive interrogation for hours, and he had to be cleaned up for the influential visitor. Farel meanwhile was entertained by Detective Sergeant Snyder, who was very curious about the state department's interest in the case.

Snyder was well aware he'd been cutting corners in his eagerness to make an arrest. He'd been encouraged to do this because the suspect had seemed so unlikely to cause any trouble; the only person behind him was his grandmother. The fact that Washington had its eye on him had come as a great shock. The interrogation, which had been unsuccessful so far in getting a confession out of Willie—though Snyder was sure it was only a matter of time—was temporarily halted.

Farel explained that he'd come representing Willie's closest living relative. Snyder wasn't interested in that. He wanted to know how the State Department got into the act. Perhaps there was some international aspect to the case he knew nothing about, something perhaps to do with secret intelligence. After all, the victim was originally Polish, and

61

Poland at present was in the headlines . . .

"Oh, nothing like that," Farel said. "It's quite simple really. My daughter goes to the same school as Willie and they're friends. As I'm working for the State Department at present, they're naturally interested in the case, too." Farel said it very solemnly. As an experienced student of Soviet affairs, he knew the value of status and the protection it could afford. Be vague; lay it on thick.

Snyder was relieved. If it had been an intelligence matter, it might have cost him the credit for an arrest, but he only had to satisfy this guy, who seemed quite reasonable and direct—he was a specialist of some kind, very scientific. Snyder had seen him once on television—he'd be satisfied with a convincing case, facts, evidence . . .

"To be honest," Snyder said in his pleasantest manner, "it doesn't look good for your young friend. He called on the murdered woman just before the murder occurred—we've got witnesses for that. Her apartment was ransacked and we found a lot of money on him. He won't explain where he got it. His fingerprints were in her apartment, and he's certainly got the hands for it. He's a very strong boy. He's also got a reputation at school for having quite a temper. Once knocked another player unconscious at basketball. Cases of strangling like this often happen in a sudden fit of rage, you know. We also have other evidence I'm not prepared to discuss at present." That was one of Snyder's favorite lines, especially with lawyers. Keep 'em guessing.

"The murder took place last night?"

"Yes, just after seven."

"He had dinner with my daughter and me last night. Mr. Alec Bruno of the State Department was also there."

"We knew he had dinner at the Tagore Restaurant, Mr. Farel, but we didn't know it was with you. He refuses to tell us much . . . so far. We checked with the manager of the restaurant. He left before seven, because the manager took a break at seven and he remembers he had left before then. He's so big he's easy to remember."

"He was going to take my daughter home—"

"He did. By cab. We've already interviewed the cab driver. The cab dropped him not far from the murdered woman's apartment."

"He denies killing the woman?"

"They always do at first."

"Has he got a lawyer?"

Snyder said, open-faced and frank, lying, "He didn't want one, Mr. Farel."

"What's his legal status at present?"

"We've not charged him yet. He's being held on suspicion. But it's only a matter of time before he cracks."

"He must have a lawyer," Farel said gently. "Perhaps the State Department can recommend a good criminal lawyer— or the Justice Department . . ." He let Snyder absorb that one for a few moments. "Now, I'd like to see him for myself."

Willie had always seemed a good-natured youth, kind to Virgie. His height was always an easy subject for conversation—they never talked much beyond that. As soon as Farel saw him now, standing on those immense, stilt-like legs in a bare back room, looking sullen and resentful, Farel realized how little he knew him. This wasn't a simple good-natured youth, but a complex, cornered man. The old ever-ready shy smile was gone and didn't reappear once all the time Farel was trying to get him to talk.

At first Farel worried that the room was bugged, that Snyder would pick up all Willie's private revelations, but it didn't take long for him to realize it didn't matter if the room was bugged or not—Willie wasn't going to tell him anything.

Willie had a bruise on his right cheekbone; he looked drained, his skin gray. There was a scared expression in his eyes. He wasn't pleased to see Farel and greeted him as if he

63

were part of a trap—just another white man.

"Your grandmother asked me to come," Farel said.

"I don't want her involved in this."

"You can't stop it. She's very worried about you."

"She's got worries enough."

"You're in serious trouble, Willie. Tell them the truth, the whole truth, Willie. That's your only chance."

"I guess I lost the basketball scholarship now. Things were going too good. I should've known."

"You haven't lost it if you didn't kill her." He couldn't help looking at Willie's big hands. "Where did you get the money, Willie?"

A glint of resentment in his brown eyes.

"If you've got an explanation, give it to them."

"I can't."

"Why not?"

He didn't answer.

"Willie, this isn't the time to hide anything."

The sullen, angry black face stared at him. No answer.

He doesn't trust me, Farel thought, frustrated. This wasn't his kind of work, dealing with human beings. It was too inexact, too subjective, too dependent on the unreliable human factor. It was the kind of front-line work the CIA specialized in, open to all kinds of errors of judgment. He had a sudden yearning to be back in his study, completely in control, searching for evidence among inanimate files and clippings rather than in the human heart. But he gave it another try.

"Have you any idea, Willie, why your teacher was killed?"

The great body squirmed restlessly, but he said nothing.

"She seems to have been kind to you."

The eyes flashed. Farel had touched a nerve like a probing dentist.

"Wasn't she kind to you? She gave you extra lessons."

No reaction this time.

64

"Willie, you can trust me. Tell me all that you know. I can help you."

Nothing doing.

"I'll get you a good criminal lawyer."

"I don't want no lawyer."

"You need one. You don't have to tell the police anything until you've talked to a lawyer."

"I don't want to talk to no lawyer."

"Well, what do you want?" Farel asked, exasperated.

"I want a basketball scholarship. That's all I ever wanted, Mr. Farel."

Farel got up, baffled. But he couldn't leave the boy like that.

"Willie, in Estonia, where I come from, we have a folk hero who walked across the largest lake in Estonia, Lake Peipus, all the way to Russia, and single-handed he brought back a load of timber. It's an exploit that's been celebrated for hundreds of years!" Willie didn't look impressed; his sullen expression didn't change. "But," Farel said, "he didn't walk *on* the water. The water was shallow in places and, like you, he was lucky enough to be very tall. Big men can accomplish big things. Don't give up, Willie."

Willie didn't reply, just looked.

"I'll be back."

Both Virgie and Willie's grandmother were waiting for him.

"Willie won't talk to me," he told them. "He knows something, but for some reason he won't tell. They found a lot of money on him. He won't say where he got it. They suspect it came from the dead woman's apartment."

"Willie brings me money often," Willie's grandmother said. "He works in a supermarket after school, he says."

"Why didn't he tell the police that?"

"I don't know, Mr. Farel. Willie is strong-minded like his

65

father was, before he got himself killed in Vietnam. He has his own way of doing things."

"What are you going to do, Leo?" Virgie said.

He pretended not to know what she meant. "What I always do at this time, go to bed!"

"What about Willie?"

"I've been to see him. I'm getting a criminal lawyer for him. There's nothing more I can do, Virgie."

"A lawyer won't find out who really did it."

"That's the police's job."

"They've got Willie. They're satisfied. The only way to save Willie is to find the real murderer."

"Virgie," he said patiently, "I can't drop everything. The State Department and the president are waiting impatiently for the result of my analysis. It may determine American policy toward Poland and the Soviet Union in a crisis situation."

"If you can find out what the Russians are doing, it should be easy to find out a little murderer," Virgie insisted obstinately. "Isn't that right, Mrs. Lee?"

"I know Mr. Farel can do it. He's the only one who can save my Willie now."

Farel sighed. "Very well. I'll tell you what I'll do. I have promised Mr. Bruno I'll try to complete my analysis by tomorrow. I must keep that promise. But instead of keeping Henrik to help me, I'll send him out to find the answers to some questions that will help Willie."

"Henrik?" Virgie said, disappointed.

"Yes, Henrik is an excellent researcher. He is skillful at finding the answers to questions."

"In the files. Answers from people are different."

"I will give him the questions to ask."

"What will you do with the answers he brings back?"

"I will analyze them to find the murderer."

66

Henrik wasn't keen on his new assignment. He was used to the study—working there alone with Farel was almost like being back in Estonia. He had lived the first part of his life very securely and easily; he hadn't had to struggle for anything. He had been middle-aged when he'd been uprooted; he'd found it impossible to readjust successfully to a new, entirely different way of life in New York. Luckily the money he brought with him allowed him to live modestly, and his work with Farel gave him an interest, a hobby. He wasn't keen to go out and interview a lot of Americans, but Farel was the boss.

Farel had already clipped the stories about the murder from the morning papers. The *Times* had only a brief inside story, but the *Daily News* spread it across three columns: GOLDEN-HEARTED SCHOOLTEACHER STRANGLED! It described the four people who had discovered the body. Farel gave Henrik the clippings to read and also described his meeting with Willie.

"Now let us take it in sequence," he said. "You better take notes, Henrik."

Henrik picked up his notebook and pen.

"First, the victim—Ursula Rogal. What kind of a woman was she really? So far we have an impression of someone who was too good to live. Goodbye, Miss Chips! We must be able to see the real woman. The motive may become clearer then. If you approach the neighbors correctly, they may be more willing to talk. With some, it might be useful to pose as a representative of her relatives in Poland . . . or as an investigator for an insurance company—do they pay out on life insurance if you're murdered? Anyway, Henrik, I'll leave it to your own good sense to decide which role to play. Only try to get us closer to the truth about this Ursula Rogal. Talk not only to her neighbors but to her fellow teachers and her students. Was Willie the only one to receive extra teaching?

67

I sense something there. Willie's attitude toward her is ambivalent. Why?

"That takes us to, second, Willie himself. We have still to bear in mind that he could have done it, although I'm increasingly skeptical. A murderer would surely do more to avoid incriminating himself. Willie's silence makes him look guilty. But if he won't talk himself, then we must find out the truth from other people. Talk to some of his friends at school. You could tell them you're representing the lawyer defending Willie. Try to find out where his money comes from—does he really work for a supermarket? Do they know anything about Willie's attitude toward the dead woman? The key may be there, Henrik.

"Now, third, the four people who found the body. If Willie didn't do it, then they must be among our suspects. The old superintendent—find out more about his background. He emigrated from Europe like she did. Did he have any secret interest in Miss Rogal? Some of those old supers are not beyond lusting after their tenants. Miss Rogal was not a bad-looking woman if the newspaper pictures are truthful; she was only in her mid-forties. Didn't she have any sex life? If so, who with? That old woman next door, Vera Charles, might know or at least have some valuable suspicions. She's probably above suspicion herself, but check out how strong she is, just in case. Check also on her identification of Willie as the caller Miss Rogal admitted. How sharp is her hearing? Perhaps she only assumed it was Willie because he had called earlier. Put it to her very aggressively—be ruthless."

"I'll do my best, Leo," Henrik said. It was hard to imagine the elderly, scholarly man being that "ruthless," but he was in fact relentless in his pursuit of a fact in the study, and Farel guessed he would be the same in the street. All Henrik needed was direction. He'd lost the will to direct himself.

"Mr. Rivera could have been more than the friendly neighbor he describes. Perhaps they were having an affair

68

that went wrong. Masseurs must have very strong hands. And Father Joyce is not above suspicion. Priests are as capable of murder as anyone else. I want to know as much as possible about their backgrounds, their characters."

He gave Henrik expense money so he could take cabs and save time, then at last he had the study to himself. Peace and silence prevailed. It was a relief to get back to his real work, and because he was so enthusiastic, the research seemed to go very easily and successfully. Even the routine chores he would normally have left to Henrik were full of interest. Facts had a cold, perfect, unchangeable beauty impossible to find in shifting, ever-changing, emotional human relationships. That was what he needed from Henrik—facts: dates, times, occupations, birthplaces—and then the work of analysis could begin. But he mustn't let this trivial case distract him. What men like Bruno, distracted by the trappings of federal power, still didn't appreciate was that the drama of intelligence work had shifted away from the point of collection, whether it was through old-fashioned human spies or the new technological spy satellites and electronic monitoring devices. The real drama now was right here, where all the data was subjected to the study of synergisms, the discovery of pieces of information that enhanced each other when brought together. If one fact had a beauty of its own, how much more beautiful were two related facts. In isolation, a fact might even seem trivial, but connected, leading to a conclusion, ah, then they had power as well as beauty. And that was what he had achieved with the facts assembled in front of him . . .

Farel worked hard and successfully all morning. Example after example fitted in and confirmed his earlier findings. By early afternoon there was no doubt in his mind. Surely Defense Intelligence would soon be able to report actual troop movements across the Polish border. He even came across a short report from Moscow that the Polish minister of national defense had flown there—that seemed to be another giveaway. The reason given was that he was among the speakers at the funeral of the old Soviet hero of World War Two, Marshal Pechko, in Red Square ("Esteemed comrades, dear Soviet friends: Deep grief has engulfed us all. Inexorable death has taken away an ardent Communist, an outstanding party official and statesman, a distinguished and gifted military leader. . . .") That item alone would have aroused Farel's suspicions. Marshal Pechko had no career or personal connections with Poland and had been retired for over twenty years. In the context of all the other evidence, it was obviously a cover to get the Polish minister of national defense to Moscow for high-level talks. He was probably being given the army's plans in detail—the bad news.

Farel sat back; he had enough data now, more than enough. Only his perfectionism drove him to amass more. It wasn't necessary. There was enough here to convince even the CIA and the Pentagon.

He phoned Bruno at the Waldorf, but he was out. Farel left a message for him to come at six.

Now that the Polish analysis was over, he was keen to make up for lost time on his researches into the current Chinese leadership. Recent contradictory statements suggested another power struggle was looming in Peking, the fifth since Mao's death. Leo had a mound of data to digest. But before he lost himself in that, he had to take a short break, recharge the batteries. The memory of Willie kept distracting him. He needed some background data there, too. He could wait until Henrik returned and send him to the library on Forty-second Street, but he decided to get out for some fresh air before Bruno arrived—he would go to the library himself!

It was like a half-day off. He enjoyed the atmosphere of libraries, the sense of all those billions of facts logically assembled and expertly cross-referenced, readily available with a minimum of human interference and possible error. He had to force himself to leave when he'd collected all the books he wished to borrow: *The Psychology of Giants, Black Teenagers in the Seventies, A Key to College Basketball, The Sexual Drive of Young Adults, The Problems of Middle-Aged Women,* and *Inside the Police.* The books contained more opinions than facts, but by speed-reading through them at a rapid rate, he might find the data he was looking for. At least he wouldn't waste much time.

Walking past Bryant Park behind the library, Farel noticed a lean black youth in a faded corduroy jacket chanting, "Loose joints," to any passerby under forty—he passed over Farel. Farel stood and watched him until the youth grew uneasy and walked away. He thinks I might be an undercover cop, Farel thought, though his sales pitch had been quite open. Paranoia must flourish in that business. It suddenly occurred to him where Willie's money had come from.

When he reached home, Virgie was cooking and he asked her if Willie had ever mentioned selling drugs.

"Not that I remember, but I know he felt it was up to him to earn some money. His grandmother has a lot of kids, and he's the eldest living with her."

The Psychology of Giants stated that exceptionally tall people were often treated as freaks even by their families, and this often created in them aggressive tendencies or withdrawal symptoms. What had been the effect on Willie? Willie was right, according to *The Psychology of Giants,* in putting six feet seven inches as the generally accepted pass mark for a male giant, and that was a sign he'd been studying the subject.

"Has Willie many friends?"

"Most of his time is spent playing basketball. I guess he's friendly with the guys he plays with."

"Has he any girl friends?"

"Willie's very cautious," she replied seriously. "He says

71

he's shy, but I think it's more that he's careful. Basketball comes first. He doesn't want to get a girl pregnant and then blow his basketball scholarship. He was very critical of a friend who gave up college when his girl was going to have a baby. He thought they should've waited."

"Willie's a very serious young man." He remembered Willie saying, *That's all I ever wanted, Mr. Farel.* Basketball! He must read *A Key to College Basketball* next. How could anyone take putting a ball through a hoop so seriously—as seriously as he took kremlinology! "It's hard to lay off the girls at his age." *The Sexual Drive of Young Adults: A Survey of Males and Females Under 21 in Five Major Cities* gave statistics for the males and females who had had their first sexual experience before the age of sixteen (a sexual experience being defined as "impregnating or being impregnated"). *Black Teenagers in the Seventies: Results of a Survey of 1,252 Young Men and Women in Twenty-Four States* estimated the number of black youths who were fathers by the age of eighteen . . .

"Some of the girls chase Willie. His height turns them on. One girl called him King Kong."

He looked at his daughter. She was growing up all the time, too fast for him to keep up. Of course Lolita had been her age, but that was only a story and it had been written in the fifties; American children now had twenty years more sophistication to feed on.

"They see him as a giant stud. They think—"

"I can imagine what they think, Virgie. It's what Willie thinks that interests me. It may explain what he is holding back. I've been reading a book about *The Sexual Drive of Young Adults.* It explains that when a boy loses his father early as Willie did, he is more susceptible to the influence of older people outside—"

"Leo, you're talking about Willie as though he's a Soviet statistic. He's a flesh-and-blood human being."

72

"No, no, you miss my point. That may explain Willie's relationship with the dead woman, how it may have developed into rather an unhealthy relationship."

Bruno arrived, ready to return to Washington; all thought of Willie had to be put aside. Leo presented his conclusions.

"Are you satisfied?" Bruno asked him immediately.

"Everything confirms it. No other conclusion is possible."

Bruno looked very grave. "That gives the president quite a problem. It means another Hungary, another Czechoslovakia—maybe worse, because the Polish workers are so militant—unless the Soviet army can be stopped. And how can you do that without a world war, Farel?"

"It's not my problem," Farel said irritably. "I can only make the analysis. I can't be responsible for the consequences."

"You don't think there's any chance you're mistaken?"

"Bruno, how can you ask that? You know my methods. I showed you some of the evidence. Another kremlinologist would have reached a conclusion much earlier. But I wanted to be sure. I'll stake my reputation on it now."

"I'm sorry." Bruno's hand trembled on his briefcase. "We're of course very grateful . . ."

"I understand your position. The messenger with bad news is unsure of his reception."

Bruno shook hands with Farel, his hand soft and cold. "At least we'll get the bad news to the president first."

9

Hinds had arrived from Paris the day before.

He phoned Dober from the airport. "Hello, old buddy. I'm to be your house guest for the duration."

The lonely life at once seemed more attractive. Dober didn't like Hinds. A small hairy man with quick hands, a Hungarian originally who never got his American ways quite right, Hinds had no class. He enjoyed violence; he couldn't talk sensibly about anything except sports and money. But he was a useful man to have with you if things went wrong. Washington must have the same uneasy feeling I have, Dober thought.

It was also like Washington to send in Hinds from outside rather than just instruct him to use someone local. Agency paranoia—and rivalry with the other intelligence branches—made it impossible now to trust anyone at the embassy. If you could infiltrate them, they could infiltrate you. Washington was now looking for Ivans of its own everywhere. When the Polish situation quieted down, all the front-line people would be reexamined, many of them purged. And then the Agency would start again, half trusting the top embassy people for a short time, then not trusting anybody local except their own imports, then maybe not even the imports . . .

Hinds' arrival probably meant they didn't trust him now,

or at least that the Ivan business was so important they couldn't risk letting him handle it alone. Dober resented the idea of a Hungarian checking up on him. He was a snob with regard to ancestry. In the bicentennial year, he had traced his family in America back a hundred and fifty years. He was more an American than Hinds would ever be. And his long experience with the Agency surely proved his complete loyalty.

But if that was behind Hinds' sudden arrival, it showed how jittery Headquarters had become.

And that made him even more uneasy.

As the time for their meeting approached, Dober kept a careful check on Ivan's activities. The Russian had arranged to see the nightclub singer the evening before, but he hadn't showed up. That wasn't unusual. If he suspected the Soviet embassy was checking up on him, he didn't take any chances. That morning he had acted as a messenger between the military attaché and a Soviet contact in the Swedish embassy. They had met with apparent casualness in a restaurant. Ivan, Dober's tail reported, looked in good shape.

The time passed for cancelling the meeting.

Dober phoned his wife before leaving and tried to make it sound casual. She went on and on about Berlin. She made it seem like the loneliest place on earth, a spiritual no-man's land, though they had once had a good time there when they went for a weekend. No, she hated it now; so did the kids. Well, when the kids were old enough, they could be left behind in school back home. She didn't listen. It was unlike her to complain so much. Maybe it was her indirect way of conveying how much she missed him, but as she went on and on, he became suspicious. She was laying it on too thick. What had she gotten into?

"When are we all going to be together again, Frank?"

"Soon, but I don't know when."

He must have sounded offhand, because she suddenly

wanted to know where he'd been, whom he'd seen, and he realized with surprise that she was nervous about him, that she was afraid he might be seeing someone else. Because of their age difference, he'd always worried their marriage wouldn't last and she'd go off with a younger man. It had never occurred to him that she had her fears, too. It pleased him.

He said gruffly, "This will all soon be over, Clara . . . one way or the other."

He couldn't say much, even if he had wanted to, because the phone must be tapped.

"Look after yourself."

"You, too."

The phone clicked—Warsaw and Berlin were separated again.

"Always been glad I'm not married, old buddy. Saves a lot of trouble in our business." Hinds sat cleaning his gun, watching a stupid cartoon on TV. It was a wonder he didn't chew gum and wear a Stars and Stripes in his lapel, Dober thought irritably. The only woman who would marry him would be a damn masochist. And the Agency sent *him* to check up on *me!* Well, you don't know for sure, he told himself. There was enough tension without creating any more between them.

"Hinds, I'll go over again with you the underground arrangements in case of trouble . . ."

The rain-slicked cobblestone street was too deserted.

All Dober's suspicions flared up.

"Park the car farther down the street," he said as he got out. "It'll be too conspicuous near the church."

"Good luck, old buddy," Hinds said.

The street was too quiet—too silent, too shadowy. He had never seen it so lifeless.

Dober slowly began to walk toward the church. His nerves were jumping. All the stores and houses had eyes. Why were there no people about?

He was sure he was being watched. Years of tension had made his instincts acute. Maybe they were on to Ivan; maybe he was walking into a trap now . . .

He made the door of the church. He glanced back at the car parked down the street—it seemed a long way off.

At first he thought nobody was inside. All the benches seemed empty. Then a shadow stirred halfway down the aisle, against the wall, and he saw Ivan.

Relief flooded in.

Ivan had made it.

It had all been imagination, paranoia caught from Washington. All his confidence came back. This was just going to be a routine pickup. Hinds had come for nothing.

Dober walked down the aisle, as slowly as a believer, carefully examining the rest of the church. He couldn't see anyone else. He edged into the bench behind Ivan and sat down. Ivan was wearing an expensive new fur coat. He had the poise, the style of a Western playboy.

"You're on time," Ivan said, smiling, as relaxed as ever. Even his smile looked expensive.

"You're early," Dober said and suddenly he sneezed—the musty smell of the church irritated his sinuses. He saw Ivan's hand tense on the bench—he wasn't so calm after all.

"I've got some shopping to do. Did you bring the money?"

Dober passed over a fat white envelope.

Ivan carefully counted the banknotes—he wasn't very trusting.

"Did you bring what I want?"

Ivan gave him a sarcastic smile, enjoying keeping him waiting, and for a moment Dober thought Ivan wasn't going to come through.

"Moscow has decided to stay out."

It wasn't what Dober had expected, but it came as a great relief.

"You mean the Soviet army's not coming back?" He wanted to be sure.

Ivan said impatiently, "That's right."

"What's the reasoning behind it?"

"Détente—trade—is more important at present. Even if there's a new, more liberal government, it won't last long. Poland can be temporarily controlled at long range. If not, the army can go back later. But the advantages gained from détente can't be risked—they are of paramount importance at present." Ivan buttoned up his fur coat, ready to go. "Okay?"

"Okay," Dober said. "You're sure of this?"

"The ambassador brought the news back. He told me personally this morning. If the decision had been the opposite, there were certain cultural events I had recommended we should cancel. He told me not to bother, to go ahead. It was confirmed in a couple of coded messages I saw." He pulled up his fur collar. "We better not be in contact for a few weeks. They'll check up on all of us to find out where the leak came from. It's too important."

"How will they know?"

"By the attitude your government takes."

"Maybe we could fake it."

"Not in an election. Your president will want to take full advantage of it if he can."

That was true; Dober couldn't deny it. The Agency's urgency reflected the president's attitude.

"You'll be safe?"

"Yes, I wouldn't risk my life just for this." He patted the pocket in which he'd slipped the envelope.

The church door behind them opened. They both looked back, tense. A burly, middle-aged man in a light raincoat

78

entered slowly, knelt for a short time, and then, crossing himself, went out again.

"Looked like a cop," Dober said.

"You're too nervous. Cops don't look like cops anymore. And even cops pray—some of them." Calm, poised, completely unworried, Ivan stood up. "I must go. It's been nice talking to you, as you Americans say." He nodded to Dober, staring him in the eyes. It meant something, that look, but Dober didn't know what. The Russian was an enigma to him. It was like trying to work out the psychology of Judas. Except that he'd come to half-like Ivan. Partly it was because he'd delivered, he'd kept his word; partly it was his damn playboy charm. You couldn't help liking the bastard.

"Goodbye, Ivan. Good luck."

He watched the tall Russian stride quickly down the aisle, open the door, and disappear.

He'd wait a few minutes and then leave himself.

Suddenly he heard voices outside, several long whistles, and then a familiar popping sound—gunshots.

Trouble. Big trouble.

He'd been right from the beginning. It was a trap.

He couldn't help Ivan now. Top priority was to tell Washington.

There were more popping sounds and then . . . silence.

He took out the pocket transmitter he always carried on a pickup. "Soviet out," he said in the code he'd arranged. "Soviet out." Headquarters would know Ivan's message in a few minutes.

Then he was free to get away—if he could.

He opened the church door just wide enough to peer out. A small group of men stood in the cobblestone street near the church. One of them was the man in the light raincoat. They were standing round something, somebody, lying on the ground. When one of the men, who looked like Russians, moved aside, he saw the fur coat. It was Ivan lying there, and by the indifference of the men standing over him, Dober concluded he was dead. He hoped he was.

The car was still where he'd left it. Hinds was sitting casually behind the wheel as if he had no part in what was happening. The car looked a very long way off.

Dober opened the church door wider and walked out. He moved casually toward the car, then when someone shouted at him, he began to run, aware he was an easy target. He heard the engine roar and the car came rushing to meet him. Hinds was risking getting hit, too. Another voice shouted and a popping sound came from behind him. He tensed but felt nothing. They were bad shots or this was his lucky day. Just as he was reaching the car, panting, out of condition, he felt a tearing pain in his left arm. A hit!

Hinds threw open the door and pulled him in. Hinds turned the car expertly, the tires squealing, and then they were roaring down the street, bouncing on the wet cobblestones, away from the guns. Both of them heard a car start up behind them.

"Make for the workers' barricades," Dober panted, holding his arm. The blood was soaking through his coat sleeve. It looked worse than it was; they might get away with it yet. "Tell them on the radio. They'll take care of the car behind . . ." A red mist was seeping into his head—he was going to lose consciousness. Hinds would be on his own. "Listen . . ."

"Relax," Hinds said. He had his gun in his lap. "I told them as soon as I saw your Russian buddy get it. That was Ivan?"

"Ye-ah."

Stefan, now Ivan—the price was rising, too high.

Maybe even Hinds and him if his emergency plan didn't work . . .

Hinds was a good guy in spite of everything . . . a good guy . . .

80

The red mist filled his head, but he put his head out the window and let the cold night air help him hold onto consciousness. He was out of condition for this kind of direct action, slowed down by a station chief's easy life. Too many meetings, too many cocktail parties . . .

The car behind seemed to be gaining, but they hadn't far to go now.

10

Henrik visited the old super first. A large bloated face peered round the door. "What d'you want?" a sleepy voice grunted. At the back of the house a dog growled.

Henrik ignored Farel's advice about playing roles. Leo had a romantic side; Henrik felt he understood the realistic ways of America better than Farel. "I represent Leo Farel," he said firmly, "the kremlinologist."

The old super, half asleep, heard "criminologist," and he assumed the dignified Henrik was some kind of police investigator. "You'll be wanting to see her room," he said, rubbing his face awake. "This way up."

He led the way like a drunken guide, swaying on the stairs and making hard labor of fitting the key in the lock. In the still dishevelled room, he proudly pointed out where the body was found. "The face was all bruised and swollen, the eyes bulging . . ." Clothes, books, the contents of drawers were still on the floor, although someone—the police?—had sorted through them and made neat piles. A Polish newspaper was on the top of one pile; Henrik pocketed it when the old super wasn't looking. He also noticed an airmail envelope with a Polish stamp, and he made a note of the sender's name and address in Warsaw.

"That's her relatives," the old super grunted. "Maybe she's left her money to them."

"She was wealthy?"

"She was a teacher." The old super said that as if he thought teachers earned a fortune.

"The newspaper said you were outside at the time of the murder."

It was a story the old super now knew by heart. "I saw Miss Rogal go in, and then I went to the john. I was also away for a few minutes feeding my dog, the one you heard growling. The murderer must have gone in during that time, robbed and killed her, and come out again. Very fast."

"Is it possible?"

"Remember he's young and an athlete. I must have missed seeing him by seconds. He took a big chance. But he was a fool, didn't think. Must have killed her on the spur of the moment—bound to be caught. And she was giving him extra teaching, being kind to him! Some of these teenagers have no mercy in their hearts today. They'll do anything for money."

"Did you see anybody else go in?"

"Later, yes. The priest—Father Joyce, he was calling to see her—and then Mr. Rivera. Both of them were with me when I found the body. It was as though we felt something was wrong. She wasn't a bad looker. Her boobs could work up any man, even an old geezer like me. But she looked ugly when she was dead. Her throat—"

Henrik said quickly, "Did she have many visitors?"

"Not that I saw. She was a quiet woman. No wild parties, nothin' like that. Not the kind you'd think would get murdered."

"Did she often talk about Poland?"

"No, only time I remember was during the recent troubles. She said she was worried about her relatives there."

"Are you from Poland, too?"

The old man looked at him slyly. "What d'you mean?"

"You emigrated from Europe, didn't you?" Henrik said clumsily as the old man scowled. "Like me. I'm Estonian."

"I'm an American," the old man growled. "Who did you say you were?"

Vera Charles opened her door at once. She'd been listening. "I thought it was Rivera," she said. "He always appears when the old super's next door. He can't keep away." She looked meaningfully at Henrik. She trusted him immediately —maybe it was his age and his courteous manner. He was her idea of a gentleman. She invited him in at once.

Her apartment was very clean and orderly and well furnished. It hardly looked lived in. Henrik sat uneasily on the edge of a chair, not wishing to disturb the perfectly positioned cushions, while she remained standing in the center of the room, small and sturdy and aggressive, reminding him of a bantam cock ready to fight.

Several rings flashed on her small, gesticulating hands as she talked, showing him a picture of her dead husband on their honeymoon in Atlantic City, introducing him to her large, leafy plants that stretched from floor to ceiling by the window, healthy, neat, all with names: "This is Paula . . . Benjamin . . . Franklin . . . Eleanor . . . I used to have animals, cats and then dogs, and I tried birds—a parrot, lovebirds— but plants are so much cleaner and human. When I talk to them, they listen. Don't you, Paula darling?"

It was with difficulty that Henrik changed the subject to the murder, but once diverted from the domestic scene—her dead husband, the plants—Mrs. Charles gave her account with great gusto and said she was looking forward to being a star witness in court.

"I was the last one to speak to her—and I heard him arrive. The police have caught him, thank God. At least we won't have him running around killing more people."

"It was lucky you heard him," Henrik said politely.

"Yes, I just happened to be near the door. I recognized his voice immediately."

84

Henrik asked casually, "Was that because he'd been by earlier?"

"I suppose so, yes."

"Have you ever talked with him?"

"Oh, no. He's not my kind of person. Oh, not at all. But I've passed him on the stairs. He had to lower his head or he'd have bumped it on the ceiling. He's very big and black. People like that, who grow so big, weaken their brains, you know. They're often mentally deficient. I'd have been scared to be alone with him in my apartment. I really would."

Henrik didn't mind asking hard questions in the pursuit of facts. "If you've never talked with him," he said nervously, "how can you be sure it was him?"

"Some things you just know," she said firmly. "I may have heard him talking to her at some time—I don't remember. But there was no doubt in my mind, no doubt at all, who it was. I told the plants"—she gave a friendly look at the tallest plant curling across the ceiling—"didn't I, Paula?"

"Did Miss Rogal have any other men callers?"

"Sometimes she would see Mr. Rivera—either in her apartment or his."

"Were they close friends?"

"I think it was closer than he told the police. But it was all very private and behind closed doors." She frowned, thinking. "There was something about her I didn't understand. I think that's why she kept me at a distance. She had something to hide . . ."

Shrieks of laughter came from Al Rivera's apartment. At least someone was in. Henrik listened. It sounded like a man and a woman. When he pressed the bell, the laughter stopped at once, but it was a long time before anyone came to the door. Rivera opened it a crack, showing his bare, hairy chest and the well-developed shoulders and arms of a weight-lifter. He obviously didn't intend to let Henrik in.

85

"I've told the police everything."

"Can I ask you a few questions?"

"There's nothing more to tell. I was one of those who discovered the body."

"The superintendent said he saw you come in. Did you pass anybody suspicious on the stairs?"

"Nobody. It's a very quiet house. I've seen that student of hers several times—he's so big you can't miss him!—but I didn't see him that day. I didn't see anybody. I've told the cops all about it. I don't want to go over it again. Ask them, man."

The door began to close.

"I understand you and Miss Rogal were close friends," Henrik persisted.

The door widened again.

"What are you getting at?"

"You and Miss Rogal—"

"We were neighbors. Get it?" Rivera said angrily. "We lived in the same house, right? Sometimes—not often—we stopped and talked for a few minutes. Why not? But if you're suggesting anything more, man, you're dead wrong."

He noticed Henrik examining his big, well-developed, well-manicured hand on the side of the door, and the hand disappeared.

"No," Henrik began, "You misunderstand—"

"Look, mister, will you stop bothering me?"

The door slammed in Henrik's face.

He met Father Joyce coming out of the church. They walked over to the house behind it. The priest was shorter than Henrik, and he looked very tired. There were dark bags under his eyes.

"We had a sudden death during the night," he said. "Not a murder this time, I'm glad to say," he added with a grave smile. "A sudden heart attack. He was gone before I could

86

get there. Heart disease is still the biggest killer of all, they say."

Henrik emphasized that Farel knew Willie. The priest would probably be more sympathetic to that.

"Have the police actually charged him with the murder?" Father Joyce asked in a rather harsh Irish accent, showing Henrik down a dim hallway to a combined sitting room and bedroom. A Bible was open on a table—at the Book of Revelations, Henrik noticed. "It's a terrible thing. Are they quite sure he did it? He's so young, but young people seem to grow up so fast in New York. Back where I come from in Ireland, some of the grown men are more innocent than the kids here. But I wonder what pushed him over the edge and drove him to it. Perhaps Miss Rogal found him taking some money. He's a poor boy, I understand, and money can be a big temptation at that age—even a few dollars. We've several times had our poor box broken into by teenagers. I'd like to help you, of course, but I don't see how I can. I've never met the boy."

"Going back to that day, Father Joyce . . ." Henrik hesitated. The priest was tired and Henrik wanted to spare him any unnecessary questions.

"Yes?"

"When you were going into the house, did you see anybody?"

"No, he must have got out before then. The first person I saw after the superintendent outside was Mrs. Charles, Miss Rogal's next-door neighbor. Then the superintendent went to the next floor to check she wasn't visiting with Mr. Rivera. Mr. Rivera came down with the superintendent, and by then we were all very anxious. It was as though we all felt something was wrong." The priest paused thoughtfully. "I suppose the body wouldn't have been discovered for a long time if I hadn't called on her. She'd made an appointment with me. I knew she must be there. I started to leave—I actually got halfway down the stairs—and then I decided to go back and try again."

"You were a friend of hers?" Henrik asked nervously, mindful of Rivera's strong reaction but wanting to get all the relationships clear.

"Oh, no. She was a lapsed Catholic. She was interested in coming back to the Church. I think she was a very troubled woman."

"Troubled in what way?"

"I can't tell you. She didn't talk about it. I didn't hear her confession, but that of course would be secret."

Henrik nodded understandingly. Because of his own family religious background in Estonia, he had more respect for the clergy than Farel, who came from a family of agnostics, traditional freethinkers. He also felt in the priest something he shared—the nostalgia of exile. There was a map of Ireland on the wall, a few other Irish mementoes about the room— a statue of St. Patrick, a tankard, a green hat, a copy of *Dubliners*. Henrik picked up a photograph of a young man lying on a beach.

"That is me . . . in Italy," the priest said. "I have changed, yes?"

Henrik nodded, putting the photograph down. There was little resemblance. "You were born in Italy, Father Joyce?"

"No, in Ireland . . . in Belfast. You notice my accent. The Belfast accent is not as soft as the Dublin one, though when I came back from Italy, I lived in Dublin for a time. But you don't lose the accent you're born with so easily. I went to Italy to study."

"For the priesthood?"

"I studied there and in Dublin, but I didn't become a priest until I came here. I was late in having my eyes opened. I began by wanting to be a millionaire—the American dream! But one day I decided I had to start my life all over again. I fancy that's what Miss Rogal was trying to do. It was tragic

88

she wasn't given enough time to do it—tragic! Murders like that are so absurd, so meaningless. A human life ended just for a few dollars." The priest frowned, remembering. "She talked as if she had marriage in mind. Perhaps that's why she wanted to come back to the church. She wanted a Catholic wedding."

"Did she mention anybody—any man she was involved with, anyone she wanted to marry?"

Father Joyce shook his head.

"I didn't know her long enough for that kind of conversation."

The school on the upper West Side was an old building that had been renovated. A guard was at the main door. He took Henrik down plain high-ceilinged corridors, past crowded noisy classrooms, to see the principal, a thin harried woman with graying blonde hair and a perpetual frown.

"Miss Rogal?" She played with the papers on her untidy desk as if the name made her nervous. "She died at a very inconvenient time for us all. I've had to take some of her classes myself. It's very bad publicity for the school. And now that one of her students has been arrested, it'll be dragged through the newspapers for weeks. She always seemed such a quiet, conscientious teacher. She gave me no trouble; she was never off sick. But I warned her about giving extra lessons at home. It can be dangerous for any number of reasons. It creates a special relationship. It's like labelling the student backward and may create a complex, doing more harm than good, you understand. The student may resent it or try to take advantage of the teacher, as seems to have happened in this case. I think that's all I can tell you. Now you see I'm very busy . . ."

Henrik didn't take the hint. "Did Miss Rogal have any special friends among the other teachers?"

She frowned even more, as if recalling Miss Rogal at all

89

required a great effort. "I don't think so. We're all too busy for much chitchat."

"Any of the men teachers?"

She killed that one at once. "Oh, no. They're all married."

"And her student? What is he like?"

"You'll have to ask Mr. Perry about that. He knew him best. He coached him in basketball."

Henrik, discouraged, found his way through a maze of more plain, high-ceilinged corridors to the gymnasium. A burly man about thirty, in jeans and a sweatshirt, was putting a class through its exercises. The sweat trickled off his face. He continued to direct the class as he talked to Henrik.

"Willie? Potentially a great basketball player. He's averaged thirty points and twenty rebounds a game here. He was an all-American last year as a junior. He could go on to become a pro if he gets that scholarship. It was in the bag until this. I knew something was wrong with him the last couple of weeks . . . STRETCH! . . . His game was off, like he was playing with only half his mind. He couldn't get it together. A good player's as sensitive as a racehorse . . . STRETCH! . . . Everything shows in his game. I asked Willie what was wrong. He just made an excuse—said he had a cold. He isn't a big talker. 'Right' or 'Yup' is a big speech for Willie. But it'll be a crime if he loses that scholarship."

"The police—"

"They're human; they make mistakes. Willie didn't do it —no way! I was against him getting involved with that sneaky bitch. I think that's what spoiled his game. I tried to talk to him, and I also spoke to her. Had a row with her, as a matter of fact."

"You didn't like Miss Rogal?"

"She was a sneaky bitch, that one. Maybe she was all right back where she came from—Poland—where she had roots, family, restraints. Here she had nobody. She was as phony as hell in my opinion, the kind of person that wakes up at

90

forty and thinks she has to make up for lost time. And someone gave it to her, paid her off, but it wasn't Willie." He yelled angrily at a tall, leggy youth who was beginning to slow down, "Get your ass up off that floor, Barnes!" He turned back apologetically to Henrik. "I'll be mad as hell if that woman loses Willie his basketball scholarship."

Coming out of the school, Henrik watched some of the older youths talking on a low wall. Most of them were bigger than he was. Their noisy exuberance and quick movements made him feel old, less the ardent pursuer of facts. He asked a tall black youth if he knew Willie.

"Yeah," the youth said cautiously.

Henrik explained he was working in Willie's interest. "Were you taught by Miss Rogal?"

"Yeah."

"What was she like?"

"She was okay."

"Did she ever give you extra lessons at her home?"

The youth grinned broadly. "No, man, big Willie was enough." He shifted uneasily on the wall. "Me, I need extra lessons in basketball. Willie's all right there."

"The police think he killed Miss Rogal."

"Yeah?"

"What do you think?"

The youth stood up—he was much bigger than Henrik. "Maybe she had it comin'," and he walked away with an easy loping stride into the street.

11

The emergency plan worked perfectly. The car behind was put out of action and all the right connections were made; within an hour they were safely among the workers in an enormous old cellar laid out as a hospital—the workers were ready for anything. Even the doctors and nurses wore gunbelts, and the gallows humor and cynical camaraderie reminded Dober of Vietnam in the worst days. They were clearly expecting the worst. He wished he could give them Ivan's good news, but they'd have to get it through the right channels. Washington would want to get the maximum advantage from it.

A young doctor in factory overalls cleaned Dober's wound and bandaged it. "You were lucky," he said cheerfully. "The bullet passed through the flesh, hit nothing solid."

Hinds bent over him, more sympathetic.

"How's it feel, old buddy?"

Strange to think it was only a short time ago he'd actively disliked Hinds. Now the sight of the familiar aggressive face that always needed a shave calmed him like an old friend. No more casualties. Stefan, Ivan . . . the whole scene outside the church came back to him. Well, at least Hinds and he had got away with it . . . so far.

"Do you feel up to a long journey, old buddy?"

He thought of his wife, the kids . . .

"Berlin?"

"No, D.C. They want us back there immediately . . . as witnesses. A plane's waiting for us."

Hinds didn't wait for an answer, but told one of the workers, "We're ready."

The man led them out of the cellar, up worn stone steps to a garage where a heavy truck was waiting. Dober and Hinds climbed up among piles of crates. They were soon speeding out of Warsaw going God knows where.

"What do you mean they want us as witnesses?"

"Don't worry about it now, old buddy. Get some rest."

Dober sat back among the crates. Hinds was right. There was nothing more to be done. Washington was in charge now.

He relaxed and slept.

As Henrik typed the last page of his report, Farel puzzled over a short news item from Warsaw on the front page of *The New York Times.*

A Soviet embassy official had been shot dead on a Warsaw street while, it was said, photographing a historic old church. The killer or killers had escaped. A Soviet embassy spokesman regretted the loss of a brilliant Soviet diplomat but had no other comment pending the result of the Polish police inquiries.

"Very strange," Farel murmured, ringing the story for Henrik to clip. It seemed like a gift to Soviet propaganda. Why weren't they making use of it? He expected the Soviet embassy to blame the Polish workers for the murder, as part of a campaign to justify the forthcoming return of the Soviet army. What lay behind this careful no comment?

Henrik finished typing, carefully stapled together a dozen closely typed pages of facts, and presented the pile to Farel.

Reluctantly pushing aside the *Times,* Farel carefully read the long report and then sat back, analysing it. Industrious

93

as Henrik had been, Farel was aware of all the remaining gaps. The chronology was not precise. At what time had the old superintendent gone to the john? At what time had he fed his dog? Between what times was he outside fussing over the garbage? At precisely what time did he go upstairs? Henrik had brought back twelve invaluable pages of facts, but the result was still a very blurred picture, too blurred perhaps to be sure of the murderer.

Questions without answers. Mr. Rivera, for example. Why had he become so angry at Henrik's question? Was it from guilt, fear, love of accuracy, or concern that the woman with him might get the wrong idea? And Miss Rogal—was she really planning to get married? And if so, to whom? The unanswered questions, the missing facts tantalized him.

Let's start at the beginning, he thought, with the background of the murdered woman in Poland. He consulted his address book for the legmen and researchers available there. It was really a choice between two men, Jerzy Bolinski, a freelance journalist, and Stanislaw Grotow, a teacher. Grotow was probably better for the job he had in mind.

"Henrik, send Stanislaw Grotow in Warsaw the relatives' address you copied out in Miss Rogal's apartment—it's on page two of your report. Also send him a clipping of the *Daily News*'s story of the case—I think it even includes pictures of the four people who found the body. Tell Grotow in your most elegant code to see what he can pick up from the family about her life there and what they've learned about her life here. Spell out what we want, because Grotow takes everything literally. But he'll be relieved that for once it's not political."

Farel read through the report again more slowly. The interconnections became clearer.

"I must check a couple of points with Willie . . . if he will talk," he told Henrik, who was busy filing. "Perhaps you could go over to the precinct . . . But, no, on second thought,

94

I better go myself. If he won't talk to me, he certainly won't talk to you, who are almost a stranger. But perhaps something here"—he tapped Henrik's report—"will encourage him to open up. I think these facts taken together give us a fair insight into his relationship with Miss Rogal. That may be the key."

Henrik didn't know what Leo was talking about.

Farel absentmindedly picked up the Polish newspaper Henrik had brought back from the murdered woman's apartment and idly turned the pages. Suddenly he froze. " 'Family anniversary postponed because soldier son not coming home' . . . ah, evidence wherever I turn!" But then he remembered the puzzling item in the *Times* about the Soviet embassy official who was shot: there was something he didn't yet understand. He was wasting too much time on this trivial local murder. . . .

Snyder had faked a reason for holding Willie longer— some marijuana and cocaine had been found on him, allegedly, and he was also suspected of being a supplier, Snyder told a handpicked judge who prided himself on crusading against the drug trade. A patrolman testified that he'd seen Willie selling loose joints in Central Park. Snyder also told the judge a murder was involved, but the inquiries hadn't been completed. That was enough. Willie's lawyer wouldn't be able to shake him loose from that in a hurry. The lawyer, furious at the maneuver, especially as Farel was worrying him to get Willie out of jail, told Snyder he should charge Willie with murder or let him go. Snyder just smiled. The case was building nicely, even though they hadn't yet trapped Willie into a confession.

They'd had one lucky break. A man in the next block came forward to identify Willie as the giant he'd seen hurrying away from Miss Rogal's block shortly after seven—the man had watched the start of the seven o'clock news and then had

95

taken his dog for a walk. The time of the murder had been fixed at just after seven. Apart from the medical evidence, Mrs. Charles was watching the seven o'clock news when she heard the murderer admitted, and Father Joyce arrived shortly before seven-thirty when the murder was already over.

Willie's explanation was that he'd called earlier to tell Miss Rogal he couldn't come that night because he was going to Virgie's birthday dinner, and as she wasn't in, he returned later and found police cars outside. He'd gotten scared and left. Why had he gotten scared? Willie shrugged. "I know how easy it is for the cops to involve you." He smiled at himself. "And now I got involved anyway."

Farel took a notebook with him when he met Willie in the same bare back room at the precinct.

He wrote in the notebook, "I have something private to say to you the police shouldn't hear. This room is probably bugged. Let's write instead of speaking." He added, "I will be as precise as possible and please answer the same way." He could have written more briefly in a kind of shorthand, but he wanted to make sure there was no misunderstanding.

He passed the notebook to Willie.

Willie, tense and drained, nodded, a large hand beating nervously on his knees. He seemed to trust Farel more this time.

Farel wrote, "The police think the money found on you came from Miss Rogal's apartment. You used to take money home to your grandmother from selling drugs—correct?"

"Yes," Willie wrote.

"Is that where this money came from?"

Willie hesitated and then wrote, "No."

"Where then?"

Willie shrugged.

"Please tell me. It's important."

96

"I can't."

"Why not?"

Willie shrugged, his hand beating faster.

Farel thought for a few moments. How could he put it to Willie? He should have sent Henrik—this human research really wasn't his kind of work. He wrote, "The first time you went to Miss Rogal's apartment did you and she"—in conversation perhaps he could have put it more delicately; written this way, it was bound to be too bald, too crude—"have sexual relations?"

The hand stopped beating, the high bony knees tensed. Willie stared at him open-mouthed, shocked.

All right, Farel thought, I made a mistake.

Willie picked up the pen quickly. "No."

Then he thought again and added, "Not the first time."

It was like breaking a long silence. Now Willie couldn't tell enough. He picked up the pen again. "She asked me the second time."

Farel quickly wrote, "I'm not trying to trap you, Willie, I'm just trying to understand."

Willie stared at him, nodding but not writing anything.

This was the difficult part, Farel thought. *Black Teenagers in the Seventies* couldn't help him now. "Maybe you had kept away from the girls because you didn't want to get any pregnant and risk losing your basketball scholarship. You were shy because of your height. You were frustrated. Then the chance came to have sex with an older woman. Fewer problems. She could look after herself. There was some extra strange attraction in the fact she was your teacher. You could dominate your teacher! You were also used to doing what she told you to do. Was that it?"

Willie couldn't wait to get hold of the pen. He began to write. "You . . ." Then his emotions overcame him. He looked up at Farel, pushed the notebook aside impatiently,

97

and cried furiously at him, "You don't get it. It wasn't that way at all. She paid me to have sex with her. *That's* where the money came from."

Farel tried to stop him from speaking aloud but then gave up when Willie ignored him. He let the youth bring it all out without interruption.

"The first time maybe it was like that, Mr. Farel—the way you described. When you've got a woman teacher, you always wonder what sex with her would be like. I guess all guys do. But she was so sick! She wanted to do all kind of crazy things. She wanted me to beat her—with a belt—on her ass! She thought black guys would do anything. You know, the old stud thing. After that first time, I didn't want to do it no more. But she insisted. She said she'd gotten used to being beaten when she was a kid—in some prison camp. She was real different at home to the way she was at school. People who only knew her at school would've been real surprised. The second time I didn't want to do it, but she kept pressing money on me, and I'd been laid off at the supermarket and the cops were leaning on us in the park—I didn't want to go to jail; I didn't want my grandmother to know I was sellin' drugs. She's very religious, but I like to take her some money home. Makes me feel good, more a man than if she's keeping all of us. So I took the money and did what she wanted. And I didn't stop at the second time. The money was too useful. But I got disgusted—sick of her and her demands. That last day I decided I'd give her back what money I had and tell her 'No more.' I'd risk her trying to stop me gettin' my scholarship. It was better to sell drugs than go through that shit. And the money I had on me was all I'd got to give back to her."

Willie had said it all in one long breathless outburst. He was spent and he slumped back, his long legs stretched out.

"But I didn't kill her, Mr. Farel."

Farel put away the notebook. There was no point to it

98

now. The cops probably had all that Willie had said on tape.

When he left, he saw Snyder in an inside office grinning broadly.

"Hi, Mr. Farel," Snyder called out. "How are all those Russians and Chinese doin'?"

Leo returned home feeling tired, which was as close to depression as he ever got. Henrik had left, but Virgie was still up, watching ballet on Channel 13 and waiting for him, for the news.

"Poor Willie," she said when he told her. He didn't leave anything out. "At least the police should realize Miss Rogal wasn't the beautiful character some people say she was."

"It also provides more of a motive than simple robbery. It doesn't help Willie."

"I don't agree with you, Leo. Willie looks the innocent, not her."

"That's your subjective way of looking at it, Virgie. Look at it another way—from the viewpoint of a cynical policeman who doesn't know Willie. Willie was involved with her. He wanted to get away, she wanted to hold him. Perhaps she threatened she'd make sure he didn't get his scholarship unless . . . Maybe they had a fight; maybe he lost his temper, disgusted with her and with himself. It's possible, Virgie. The police may conclude that if he could beat her—"

"On her orders for money!"

"—he could kill her."

"There's a big difference."

"To us, but maybe not to them—or to a jury. No, Willie's in trouble."

They sat in silence, thinking about it.

"Leo?"

"Yes?"

"Why does a woman like that enjoy being beaten?"

Farel took a deep breath. He always tried to give her an

99

adult answer. "There's sometimes a close relationship between pleasure and pain, Virgie. From what she told Willie, it reminded her of something that happened when she was a child, when she was most impressionable. Poland had some of the worst Nazi concentration camps. Experiences in them affected adults for life—those who survived. What must it have done to children? We know so little about it. We know much more about the sexual cult of sadism and masochism, usually referred to as S-M—psychologists have a field day with it. Some of them claim it can be a part of healthy sexual enjoyment provided it's not carried to excess, but more often it reflects a distortion in the person."

"So she made use of Willie!"

"Willie may be right. She may have had a racial hangup, too."

"I despise her!"

"You can't despise anyone until you understand them." More silence.

"What are you going to do next, Leo?"

"I want Henrik to go and ask some more questions."

"That old superintendent could have killed her. He said he went inside twice, to go to the john and to feed his dog. Maybe he went inside a third time—to kill her."

"It's possible," Farel said doubtfully. Anything was possible, but speculations weren't facts. He also didn't like the idea of her thinking about a murder so deeply—she'd be having nightmares. "Isn't it time you were getting to bed, Virgie? You've got school in the morning."

"I just want to watch the end of this program."

"Virgie, you haven't watched it once since I came home."

"Oh, all right." She got up unwillingly. "But I do hope you're going to help Willie soon."

"I'm doing my best."

"But you're not giving it your whole attention."

"Virgie, I've got other work to do."

100

"But all the time Willie's waiting—he's in jail," she said. "He's counting on you."

"Good night, Virgie."

He sat alone in the empty living room among the old furniture that reminded him of his wife, with only a table lamp on. The semidarkness was soothing.

He thought of the dead woman. Had she been having sex with Rivera, too? With his temper, he might have enjoyed beating her! Henrik must go back to find some more answers. It was no use questioning Rivera himself, but perhaps the old super or the nosey next-door neighbor . . . And had she really been turning religious at the same time? Father Joyce had concluded she was sincere. Was it guilt? . . .

What he needed was more background information. He switched on the chandelier he'd bought for his wife the first year of their marriage and picked up *The Problems of Middle-Aged Women.* I know more about the problems of middle-aged men, he thought, turning to the chapter on "Sexual Relations with Younger Men." Maybe, too, he should read something about—what was the priest's expression?—lapsed Catholics.

The phone rang.

It was Bruno calling from Washington. His heavy, ponderous voice sounded excited.

"Farel, can you do us one more favor? Can you fly here in the morning to attend an urgent meeting?"

"Impossible, Bruno. I still haven't caught up on all the lost time."

"This is very important. Your conclusion's under fire. The CIA's come up with the exact opposite from a top Soviet source."

"Well, they're wrong."

"They're flying their man in as a witness, to back it up. We need you. Tomorrow morning the National Security Council will hear each side and then decide which conclusion to support and present to the president. We'd like you to appear before it."

"I'm not a Washington man, Bruno. I've made my analysis, now it's up to you people what you do with it."

"It may mean the difference between the acceptance of your conclusion and its complete rejection."

"That would be an absurd error."

"Well, then . . ."

Farel sighed.

"Okay, you win. What time do I have to get there?"

Bruno was obviously relieved. "The meeting is set for ten-thirty. If you get the nine o'clock shuttle, I'll have a limousine at the airport to meet you. You better bring full documentation for your analysis. It may be a tough session."

12

Henrik arrived early next morning to find that Farel had already left for Washington. His instructions for the day were contained in a hastily written note on top of Henrik's typewriter.

For a moment the faithful Henrik rebelled. He didn't want to go back to question those people again! He wasn't going! "I am not a detective," he told Virgie indignantly as she was finishing her breakfast.

He found no sympathy there. "It may help Willie, Henrik," she said firmly.

Henrik eyed the piles of clippings waiting to be filed, sighed as if letting out the spirit of rebellion, and then, pocketing his research notebook, he reluctantly set off.

The old super wasn't in. Henrik was trying to decide whether to risk pressing Rivera's doorbell when he saw the old super approaching down the street with a big dog on a short leash, a young German shepherd. The old super didn't recognize Henrik until they were close, and then his little, shortsighted eyes peered and he grunted something Henrik couldn't hear. The dog growled, showing a savage mouth, and the old super cursed and struck it with the end of the leash.

"Still trainin' him," he said. "Don't want him to like

nobody but me. That way he'll be a good house dog. If Miss Rogal'd had him, she'd be still livin'.''

He didn't wait for Henrik to explain why he'd come back, but walked into the house to his apartment at the back. Henrik followed uneasily, watching the big frisky dog. It was only a few strides. He imagined the old super that day going in to the bathroom—it would take only a few minutes, but long enough for someone to get in or out . . . if he was telling the truth.

The apartment consisted of a large dirty room with a bathroom at the back. There was a pervasive smell of stale food, stale man, stale dog. The dog growled again at Henrik. The old super slapped it with a beefy hand and dragged it into the back yard and slammed the door.

"Hates people," he said, pleased, as the dog whined and scratched at the door. "Took him in Miss Rogal's apartment and he got very excited sniffing round the couch. I gave him something from the other apartments and he didn't get excited. That means it was someone from outside. I'm going to get somethin' that student touched. Bet that excites him."

He took a can of beer out of the refrigerator.

"Want some?"

"No, thank you." Henrik half bowed. "It is too early . . . for me."

"Never too early for beer. My father had it for breakfast every day. Lived to be ninety-four." The large, bloated face came closer and the eyes peered; it occurred to Henrik how easy it would be for someone to pass near the old super without being seen. "What've you come here for?" The old super's mood had suddenly changed, as if he thought Henrik had come to trap him. "I'll set the dog on you." He stepped toward the back door and the dog howled to be let in. He emptied the can and chuckled. "That scared you." His mind was like a pendulum, swinging from one mood to another. He reminded Henrik of a schizophrenic farmer he'd known back home in Estonia—the man had killed his wife in a drunken fit.

Henrik said carefully, "I have been puzzled. I thought you might be able to help me . . ." Appeal to the old man's vanity, but then what? "Mr. Rivera—he became quite angry when I asked him if he and Miss Rogal were friends."

"He did, did he?" The old super took out another can of beer; the crack when he opened it made Henrik start. "Rivera's a strange one. Women all week, church on Sunday. Spanish are very emotional people, will fight in a minute."

"And he and Miss Rogal? . . ."

"I heard them arguin' once. You don't argue like that if you ain't close. She told him he had 'a dirty mind.' I guess he'd been leadin' up to a roll in the hay. Wouldn't have said no to a bit myself." The little eyes peered dangerously, the pendulum of his mind on the move again. "But I respected the woman. You can't say I didn't. Nobody can say that— nobody!" The eyes now had a wily look. "Rivera's a cold one with women, but not me. I'm not past it, but I respect them. You want to know somethin'?" His mind was on the move again. "One of her friends came by last night. Wanted somethin' out of the apartment."

"Someone you know?"

"Never seen her before. Said she'd loaned Miss Rogal some files from her job and she wanted them back. I checked the apartment. Some files are there."

"And you gave them to her?"

"No, nothin' can leave without police permission. She was pretty angry."

"Have you got her address?"

"At her job." The old super burrowed among dirty dishes and empty beer cans on a crowded table and came up with a business card. *Ms. Frances Cernik.* The address was a well-known news magazine. Henrik made a careful note.

The old super watched him suspiciously. "Why d'you

105

want to know? What are you after?" He edged toward Henrik, peering. "What've you come here for?"

Henrik backed nervously to the door. A very unsatisfactory visit. Farel should stick to his important work. . . .

The magazine occupied several floors of one of the older midtown skyscrapers. Once very fashionable, the aging, faded building reflected the status of the magazine itself, which had once been a sensational success but was now struggling to find a new formula in the face of television's much faster reporting. Going up in the slightly bumpy elevator, Henrik felt the building, the magazine, and himself all had something in common: they were all a little passé, but were still surviving.

Frances Cernik was just the opposite. A small, neat, smiling brunette in her late thirties, she was determined to be fashionable no matter what the cost, not only surviving, but a with-it success while so many other heads were rolling. She had survived more bosses than she bothered to count. She was now a senior researcher in the foreign department of the magazine, and she knew a lot about Farel, having checked the facts in a short profile of him when his earlier prediction about Poland proved correct.

"And Leo Farel's interested in Ursula's murder?"

Henrik explained why.

"How fascinating! It'll make a story for the magazine. I'll tell—"

Henrik looked alarmed. "No, no, what I tell you is confidential. I'm sure Mr. Farel wouldn't want any publicity. I've come to see you just to check out your connection with Miss Rogal."

"Simple. I have a young son from my marriage—I'm divorced now, but that's not the point. Ursula was my son's teacher. That's how I met her. I'm part Polish, too, on my mother's side, so we had a lot in common. But I didn't see her often. I work long hours at the magazine and she was busy with homework—she was a very serious teacher. My son thought there was no one like her. That was why I wanted to meet her. We used to get together for a cocktail and a gossip about once a month."

"I understand you loaned her some files."

She frowned. "That's embarrassing. I loaned them to her on the understanding I'd get them back in a couple of days. They're not supposed to leave the building. Now I can't get them back, and with all this trouble in Poland, they might be needed any time. Of course neither of us could know she'd be murdered just after I handed them over."

"Was there anything in the files that might help to explain her murder?"

"I don't think so. Ursula told me she was studying the period of her childhood in Poland, the period of World War Two. We've got extensive wartime files—I've helped to build up those on Poland because it's a period and a country I'm interested in, too. But I don't see how that could possibly have any bearing on her murder."

"Did she say why she was studying the period?"

"Her father was killed by the Nazis, she spent some time in a concentration camp. She wanted to learn more about it. In fact, she had almost an obsession about it. Every new book about the Nazis that came out she bought or got out of the library. When I saw her last, she said she was reading a book entitled *On the Edge of Destruction* about the Polish Jews between the two world wars. She wasn't Jewish herself, but she was always interested in anything to do with Jews or the Nazis in Poland. Maybe it was part of her exile's nostalgia. Don't you feel that way about—where is your birthplace?"

"Estonia. When did you give her the files?"

"The day before she was killed. I had them delivered to her by messenger. She was in a hurry for them. I met her the next day, the day she was killed, and she was supposed to

107

bring them back then, but she said she hadn't finished with them."

"How did she seem?"

"The same as ever. We met for a cocktail after she finished school. She was relaxed and wanted to go on drinking, but I had to get back to the magazine to check a story. She went home and you know what happened. She must have been murdered within an hour after we parted. Maybe if we'd gone on drinking, she'd still be alive."

"The superintendent of her building said if she'd had a dog like his—"

"That objectionable man who wouldn't give me my files! He's a moron. He could have killed her himself."

"Why do you say that? Did she ever mention him?"

"Only to joke about him. She called him 'the Beast.' I'm not surprised. I wouldn't want to be alone with him!"

"Did she ever mention to you she was thinking of getting married?"

"She told me once she was involved with a younger man. But she didn't mention marriage."

"Who was he?"

"That was all she said. She never referred to him again. That was like Ursula. You learned not to ask her questions. She was very secretive. She never introduced me to any of her friends, but she met several of mine."

"Did you know she'd approached a local priest about going back to the Catholic Church?"

"No, she never mentioned that. It surprises me. She never seemed in the least religious to me. Quite the opposite. But it's another example of how secretive she was. Maybe she was thinking of marrying a Catholic. She said there was an attractive Spanish fellow in the building."

Her interoffice phone buzzed.

"That's my boss. Say, he knew Ursula. I introduced them and he took her out a couple of times, but keep that to

108

yourself because he's married. He was keen on her, I think
—keener than she was. Would you like to meet him?"

"I leave no stone unturned."

In a large back office with a fine view of downtown, a
plump, balding man was practising golf swings. She introduced Henrik.

The golf club paused in midair and he said testily, "Fran,
I wish you wouldn't discuss my private business with . . .
outsiders." He turned on Henrik irritably. "There's nothing
I'm prepared to say. It's a serious matter, a murder case. I
refuse to be questioned by anyone but the police, and then
I'll have my lawyer present."

Henrik retreated, grumbling to himself that Farel should
do his own dirty work.

"I'm sorry," she whispered, following him out. "We're all
tensed up around here. We're rushing a big cover story on
Poland. What does Leo Farel think's going to happen?"

13

The military plane landed in an obscure corner of Andrews Air Force Base late at night Washington time.

It was a cold, clear night, and Dober and Hinds were hustled from the plane to a jeep waiting by the side of the rough runway. A quick, bumpy ride that made Dober's arm ache took them to a black Cadillac limousine parked close to a freight road leading out of the airfield. Within minutes of landing, they were on their way.

Nobody talked. Hinds sat back with his eyes closed. Dober stared out of the window. He hadn't been home for a couple of years, but this dark landscape could have been anywhere —anywhere in the West at least. After a few miles, he noticed persistent lights following far back, and he leaned forward to tell the driver, who was hunched over the wheel. Hinds' eyes opened.

"Ours," the driver grunted without glancing back, concentrating on the dark deserted roads. The speedometer hovered between eighty and ninety. The Agency wasn't taking any chances, although such precautions weren't necessary. They weren't bringing back any secrets Washington didn't know already, Dober thought wearily, and the Russians must be aware of what they knew by now. Hinds chuckled and closed his eyes again.

Dober guessed where they were going. He recognized the

110

route to the Interrogation Center, a large lonely mansion in acres of woods near Arlington, where he'd once worked for several months. The driver was speeding now as if the car behind belonged to the Russians, and Dober realized they were short of time if the White House meeting at which they were to appear was being held that morning. There was a lot to be covered before then if the Agency was to be fully prepared.

He recognized the high chain-link fence topped by barbed wire and the sign: "U.S. Government Reservation. No Trespassing." The driver flashed his Agency badge at the guard in the gatehouse, and then they were roaring up the driveway through the woods Dober remembered so well, for it was there he had completed his training in evasion and escape and border crossing.

At the center they were taken without ceremony to the basement, where a long, draining interrogation began at once. Two men worked on them—Dober didn't know either of them, they'd been recruited since his time there. They were smooth, tough, and thorough. The interrogation covered the spotting, development, and assessment of Ivan—the three stages in an agent's recruitment—and then all that had happened up to the flight across the Atlantic. They went back and forth from many angles over Stefan's original, lengthy check on Ivan. You could never tell if they were satisfied with the answers—they just nodded, their faces after a time seeming almost interchangeable, and then they came back at you from another angle. Dober, who was used to the tricks of interrogation, was impressed by the job done on him.

After they were through with him, he listened closely to Hinds' cross-examination. They asked many of the same questions. Did he know what Ivan had told Dober? Yes, Hinds replied, Dober had told him in case anything happened and Hinds had to go on alone. Had he told the Polish

111

workers what Ivan had said? No, Hinds replied, though it was tempting to share the good news—it meant the workers would have a chance to topple the government without Soviet interference and to replace it with a freer, more liberal administration. Hinds tended to talk too much, trying to ingratiate himself with his interrogators, and they kept interrupting, cutting him short, keeping him to the point.

At last it was over.

Dober was surprised to find he was covered in sweat. This was a friendly interrogation; he'd reacted as if it were the enemy, perhaps because the outcome was so important. If the politicians in Washington were allowed to blow this, Stefan and Ivan would have died for nothing. Perhaps he'd sweated, too, because he was so tired—the strain of the getaway, the loss of blood . . .

While the tapes of the interrogation were being summarized into typewritten statements to be cleared by the director himself and then copied and distributed to members of the National Security Council before the morning meeting, Dober and Hinds were examined by an Agency doctor. Dober protested it wasn't necessary—he had only a superficial flesh wound that had been cleaned and bandaged—but one of the interrogators told him cynically, "You've gotta be made up before you go on stage."

The bandage came off and the wound was given a much more elaborate dressing. Dober's arm was then put in a sling and, because a knee-cap was bruised, he was also given a stick to walk with. He came out of the examination looking much worse than when he'd gone in, feeling faintly bogus and ridiculous. The doctor seemed disappointed he could find nothing wrong with Hinds. "Give me a black eye patch," Hinds suggested. The doctor, a small intense, poker-faced man, wasn't amused. He gave them both massive doses of vitamins and injections of XK, the latest high energy

112

substitute, to keep them wide awake for the next twenty-four hours.

Dober and Hinds were then rushed into Washington just after dawn to a CIA two-story stucco building disguised as an environmental protection institute near the Library of Congress. They were given a heavy three-course breakfast, allowed to take showers and to shave, and provided with new, pressed, sober business suits that fitted them perfectly. Then they were briefed by a top assistant to the director on the White House meeting they would shortly be attending.

The president was to be there—he'd cancelled a campaign swing through the key state of California and had flown back to Washington overnight, arriving about the time the interrogation was ending. The secretary of state, the secretary of defense, and the chairman of the Joint Chiefs would also be there, along with their assistant specialists in intelligence and Soviet analysis. Everyone at the meeting would already have read the statements prepared from the interrogation. The director of Central Intelligence would introduce Dober and Hinds, and then they would be questioned, possibly quite aggressively by the State Department representatives.

The director joined the briefing toward the end. Dober had met him only once before and then very briefly, but he greeted Dober as if he were an old friend, grasping his hand and stopping him from getting up.

"You've done a great job, Frank. I hope you're not in much pain."

"Looks much worse than it is," Dober said, embarrassed, touching his sling.

"It'll make a good impression on the meeting. You'll have their sympathy. It'll give what you have to say an extra authority. Whatever they ask you, don't get rattled or irritated. Remain calm and perfectly reasonable. That'll make an excellent impression on the president." The director put

113

a hand on his shoulder. "This'll be a great boost for us. We'll not forget you, Frank." He seemed very confident and pleased.

A lean man with bushy red hair hovered behind them. The director gestured for him to join them.

"Podz here will run through what they're likely to ask you, especially the trick questions. They'll want to kill Ivan's credibility—keep that in mind. Podz'll also tell you how Ivan's death has been reported in Poland and the Soviet Union. You can probably make good use of that. It weakens Farel's case from the start."

"Leo Farel?"

"Yeah, the kremlinologist. He's backing the idea the Soviet army's going back in. The State Department's basing their case on him. It's us or them, Frank. That's basically why you're here."

Dober looked worried. "What's Farel's evidence?"

"Nothing you need worry about. All analytical stuff— nothing hard like what you've got. How can they match what you've found out on the spot in Warsaw with what he digs up a couple of thousand miles away in New York? It doesn't make sense."

"Farel's got a good reputation. The Russians respect him."

The director put his arm round Dober's shoulders. "Let me tell you, Frank, what I told the president a short time ago. I quoted to him what Colby, when he had my job, used to say about analysts. The farther away they were 'from the smell of a problem' the more artificial was their judgment. Well, Manhattan's a hell of a long way from the smell of Warsaw. And that's what's wrong with Farel's case. It's all artificial head stuff. I just want you to go out there, Frank, and tell it like it was—like it is—like it's going to be . . ."

*   *   *

114

The president had lost weight since the last meeting of the National Security Council. Although a natural campaigner, exhilarated by the crowds that had greeted him across the nation, he was beginning to show the strain of the tough, neck-and-neck race; the latest polls still had him a percentage point behind.

In a tired, irritated tone, he told the meeting how the media at every stop had questioned him about Poland. It had developed into the big foreign policy controversy of the campaign, and the night before at a huge rally in Boston, his opponent had called for much greater support for the Polish workers and a tough ultimatum to the Soviet Union: "Stay out—or else."

" 'Or else' what?" said the president impatiently. "I don't want to respond with empty threats. The speech I'm making tomorrow night over national television must be realistic—based on our knowledge of what the Soviet Union is going to do."

"We have it straight from the horse's mouth," began the director of Central Intelligence.

"Leo Farel thinks differently," interrupted the secretary of state, "and he was right before."

"Gentlemen," said the president, staring in turn at the two rivals, "we have conflicting reports, and this morning we at this meeting"—he glanced round at all the somber faces in the Cabinet Room—"have to decide which report is correct. That's why I've cancelled some very important campaign appearances out west to return to Washington to be with you. It's vital that we reach the right decision."

Behind him, Pete Baldwin, his special assistant on national security affairs, leaned forward and whispered to him. Behind Baldwin was a whole team of specialists—on Europe, China, the Middle East, Latin America, global issues. The president nodded several times as he listened and then turned back to the meeting.

115

"Briefly, as Pete points out, it all comes down to this: who do we believe—the Soviet agent or the Farel analysis? Over breakfast I've studied the background briefing papers you all have before you, including Mr. Dober's statement and"—his eyes looked down to find the name—"Mr. Hinds', and the Bruno report on Mr. Farel's analysis. I've also looked at the Defense Department scenarios of what each means in terms of possible responses . . ."

The president was making it clear to the assembled intelligence and foreign policy experts that, unlike some of his White House predecessors, he intended to be fully in control of the intelligence network, and he would make the final decision at this highly unusual meeting.

"Now I'm ready to hear the first witnesses."

The director of Central Intelligence signalled to an assistant at the door. The Secret Service guards stepped back, and Frank Dober, who had been waiting outside for twenty minutes, made an impressive entrance in dark suit and white sling, leaning slightly on a stick. He was followed by a grave-faced Hinds. Sympathetic eyes followed them to the empty chairs facing the president.

"Gentlemen," the president said briskly, "I'm most grateful for your attendance this morning, especially as one of you has been wounded. I hope you're not in much pain, Mr. Dober."

Dober shook his head. He had an old-fashioned military man's appreciation of rank and status, and the president was the commander-in-chief. The sling and the stick embarrassed him. "I was lucky, sir."

"We'll try not to keep you long. We wouldn't have troubled you if it wasn't so urgent." The president fingered Dober's statement prepared by the interrogators. "I've read Mr. Dober's report, and the only outstanding question is whether your Soviet informant was completely reliable. If he was, then we have no problem. But can we be sure?"

116

"I think Mr. Dober is convinced of his reliability," said the director of Central Intelligence quickly. He looked at Dober. "You put him through an exhaustive check, isn't that right?"

"Yes, we checked him out very thoroughly," Dober said firmly, looking directly at the president.

"I know you covered this in your statement," the director said, "but let's go over it again briefly. How did he come to you?"

Dober said slowly, as if carefully remembering, "The access agent was a Polish journalist named Stefan Michalowski. He was active in the Polish resistance as a boy. We recruited him in the fifties, before my time there. I first had direct dealings with him during the workers' demonstrations in 1970. He sheltered one of our worker informers from the Polish secret police at great personal risk. Then because of what he saw of their methods—our informer was eventually beaten up and run down in the street—Michalowski became an obsessive worker against the Communists . . ." As he talked, Dober recalled the pinched indignant face, the tears of bitterness over the body in the street. "He became one of our best agents in Poland—the best informed . . ."

"And it was through Michalowski that you recruited Ivan?" prompted the director.

"It took over a year. Michalowski was regarded as a trustworthy journalist, and he met all the new people at the Soviet embassy. He often acted as go-between for various Polish cultural groups with the embassy. That was how he became friendly with Ivan. Ivan was one of three cultural attachés. At that time the Soviet Union was making a big play in the Polish cultural field to try to offset the cultural influence of the Catholic Church. One of the cultural attachés was no more than a KGB thug, but the other two were genuine. Ivan, a graduate of Leningrad State University—his real name was Leonid Valkonov—was a cultural attaché with second-secretary rank. The average Soviet attaché, as you

117

know, if he's not a KGB man, is a colorless bureaucrat afraid of offending the KGB watchdogs, but Ivan had a much more independent attitude and he got away with it. Michalowski soon noticed this and made a point of trying to make friends with him. He invited him to several parties in Warsaw and, much to Michalowski's surprise, Ivan not only accepted but showed up. The nature of Ivan's work made it difficult for the KGB to keep him under surveillance all the time, and Ivan took full advantage of his freedom."

"So Michalowski and Ivan saw a lot of each other?" the director said, coaxing him along.

"They were both youngish men, had similar cultural interests. Nobody could have called Michalowski a playboy"—he remembered the pinched, sallow face that seemed to match the shabby clothes—"not by any means, but he got around the city a lot, he knew a lot of people. He was very useful for introducing Ivan to the kind of social life he enjoyed, intellectual poker parties and sophisticated women, for the more Michalowski got to know him, the more Ivan revealed a playboy temperament and a wild extravagance."

"Didn't the Soviet embassy try to discipline him?"

"The genuine cultural attachés are allowed a certain ... er ... eccentricity. They have to mix with artists, all kinds of strange people. Ivan was very successful at it—at his work. His independent attitude seemed to appeal to the Poles, and he succeeded in winning a lot of Polish cooperation at a difficult time. If the price was a bit of gambling and womanizing, the embassy was willing apparently to put up with it, to be tolerant with Ivan. I guess even the Soviet bureaucrats and the KGB gorillas sometimes have a sneaking admiration for the macho type. And Ivan was a man of great charm and sophistication. We know the ambassador thought well of him. It was the ambassador who told Ivan of Moscow's decision to stay out."

"Straight from the horse's mouth," the director couldn't

118

help adding, with a meaningful look at the president and the others round the table.

Dober continued quietly, "But gambling and women cost money in Warsaw, like anywhere else, and Ivan soon ran up some pretty big poker debts, and he became deeply involved with a Polish nightclub singer Michalowski introduced him to. He was soon borrowing heavily from Michalowski— money we advanced. The idea was to encourage Ivan's extravagance as much as possible and get him so much in debt that he would be attracted by an offer to make some money —big money. When Michalowski eventually hinted he knew of ways Ivan could add to his income, Ivan was eager to hear about it. Michalowski's little scheme worked beautifully. He fell right into our net when we thought he was ready."

"Didn't it seem a little too easy?" the secretary of state asked, staring at Dober across the table, his eyes hostile. "Poker, women, gambling debts—he sounds too much like the classical rake begging to be saved, to be recruited."

"That was just my reaction," Dober replied, unruffled, very low key. "I told Michalowski I didn't even want to consider Ivan for recruitment until he'd been put through a series of extensive checkups and rigorous tests. We already knew something of his background from our coverage of his previous tour of duty in Czechoslovakia, and from what we'd picked up from a defector debriefing, from communications intelligence, from our own cultural people, and from some other miscellaneous sources within the Soviet Union. We knew that his father, a career soldier, had been imprisoned for making derogatory remarks about Stalin in a letter home to his wife and had died in a prison camp in Siberia. When Michalowski referred to this, Ivan showed he was still bitter about it—the treatment of his father. It came out over a few vodkas late at night. Michalowski suspected this bitterness affected his psyche as a Communist official, and it surfaced at an unpredictable moment of strain when Ivan found himself in debt and in love. His bitterness and his need for money played into Michalowski's hands."

"It still seems too easy a motivation—too simple," insisted the secretary of state.

"I agree with you," Dober said patiently, reasonably. "I wouldn't agree to recruit him until he passed all the agent development tests. We tried to trap him in various ways and we failed. He began to bring us valuable information."

"And the embassy suspected nothing?" the secretary of state asked sharply.

"Oh, don't think Ivan was stupidly reckless. Sometimes he cancelled meetings or didn't show up at parties because he thought it might be risky. He'd only see the nightclub singer when he was sure it was safe, and he was in love with her— I've read some of his letters and listened to tapes of them together. The man couldn't have been acting over so long a period. The woman would have seen through him. She was a beautiful woman, easy to fall in love with, and she had a temperament like Ivan's. They had a lot in common. But even with her, Ivan protected himself. He only saw her, stayed with her, when he judged it was safe—as far as he was able. It's an exposed position however you play it."

"But you still weren't satisfied?" the director said gently.

"In theory, yes—I couldn't fault him—but in practice, no. It's so rare to recruit anyone inside a Soviet embassy that I couldn't believe our good luck. I went on insisting that Michalowski put him through further tests. Michalowski became rather exasperated with me . . ." The pinched, sallow face came back to him again—Michalowski was bending over a steaming kettle in his small, poorly furnished apartment (Where did his money go to?), insisting that Ivan had been checked out enough: *We'll drive him away, Frank. We'll lose him* . . .

"You suspected something instinctively," the secretary of state challenged him. "You had professional doubts."

"No, it wasn't that," Dober replied thoughtfully. "In Eastern Europe, you soon learn to be super cautious in any matter involving the Russians. They have a lot to lose. I was just showing basic professional caution."

"How did you settle your doubts?" asked the director. "When did you finally decide to recruit Ivan?"

"I insisted Michalowski put him through another series of tests. He passed everything. The various checkups revealed nothing negative. Finally I got a polygraph in the diplomatic pouch and Michalowski tested him on that."

"Was that unusual?" the secretary of state asked.

"I'd had it done before. Also, Headquarters likes periodic polygraph tests of established agents. The only danger in a delicate situation like this one with Ivan is that he will refuse to take the test and we'll lose him. Some agents are scared of polygraph tests in case they give away more than they want to. But Ivan went along with it. He was very obliging."

The president leaned forward. "And he passed?"

"Oh, yes. Michalowski was very pleased with the polygraph results."

The president was impressed and exchanged glances with others at the table. He leaned back and whispered something to Pete Baldwin.

Dober added, "Michalowski thought that was conclusive, that I couldn't ask for more."

"So then you agreed to recruit him?" the director said.

"Yes, I told Michalowski to go ahead."

"And you were satisfied yourself?"

"Well, I couldn't argue with all the tests and the polygraph, but, to be frank, I wasn't completely happy until Ivan came through with the information about the Soviet plan to kill Michalowski."

"Tell us about it."

"Ivan informed me privately that the embassy was on to Michalowski working for us. He had been watched, his

121

phone had been tapped, and eventually he'd been careless and given himself away. The KGB decided he was too dangerous to leave active in Warsaw—he was our key man there, part of our operation would be crippled if they got rid of him; he also had too much access to their activities in Warsaw. He had to go. They also wanted to use him as a warning to other potential Polish informers. Ivan said they planned to get him to a phony meeting—he knew the place and the time—and Michalowski would never be seen alive again. The trouble was I couldn't warn Michalowski without endangering Ivan. Ivan said they'd know who'd warned Michalowski because Ivan was the only one who knew about it apart from the KGB men at the embassy. I had to choose between warning Michalowski and risking the loss of Ivan, or keeping quiet. I trusted Ivan completely by then, and I decided he was potentially too valuable to lose. So I kept quiet. I didn't warn Michalowski. His body was found in a field on the outskirts of the city, shot in the back."

Dober paused, thinking of Stefan passing the interminable line outside the new Western-style supermarket on his way to that phony meeting—the trap. There was a brief, almost embarrassed silence. Alec Bruno leaned forward to whisper to the secretary of state, who nodded and then stared across the table at Dober.

"So, if you didn't do anything about it," he said, "The information from Ivan was useless."

"That wasn't Ivan's fault," Dober said sharply, ruffled for the first time. The director glanced quickly at him, concerned, and Dober dropped back into the same unemotional, low key. "As far as Ivan knew, we might decide Michalowski was more valuable and warn him at Ivan's expense. He took a big risk."

"Why would he do that?" asked the secretary of state too quickly.

"Because he was genuine, one hundred percent genuine,"

122

retorted the director happily. "Could you ask for better proof?"

"It didn't make much difference in the long run," Dober said quietly. "They soon trapped Ivan, too. I guess their investigation of Michalowski led them to check on everybody who dealt with him. Maybe they sweated it out of Michalowski before they killed him."

"Mr. Dober," the secretary of state said slowly, "why do you think the Russians had the shoot-out at the church instead of confronting Ivan in the privacy of the embassy and dealing with him there?"

"A matter of time. They'd just got on to him. They wanted to stop him passing on any more information to us. They arrived too late. It may also have been intended as another of their not so very subtle warnings."

"Will it spoil their plans," the director asked with a confident smile, "now that we know they're going to stay out?"

"We don't know that," snapped the secretary of state. He hesitated, then added, "Not for sure." Sitting behind him, Alec Bruno looked gloomy.

"Would you like to hear from Mr. Hinds?" the director asked.

"No, that won't be necessary," the president said, glancing at his watch. "We've all read his report. He didn't have any direct contact with the Russian and that's the key."

"What more do you need to be convinced?" the director asked, looking at the president and then down the long table at the other faces. "Isn't the Russian reaction to Ivan's death a giveaway?"

"It seems that way to me," Dober said. "If the Soviet army was going back in, you'd expect the Russians to blame Ivan's death on the Polish workers as part of a campaign of justification. Their 'no comment' certainly supports the idea that they don't intend to interfere. I'm convinced Ivan was right."

"So am I," said the director.

"But can they afford to sit back and let the Polish workers take over and liberalize the government?" the secretary of state said.

"It's a calculated risk," the director replied.

Dober added quietly, "According to Ivan, the Soviet Union calculates that even if there's a new, more liberal government, it won't last long. Poland can be temporarily controlled at long range. If not, the army can go back later."

The secretary of state shrugged. You couldn't tell what he meant by it.

The president said briskly, "I'll reserve judgment until I've heard the next witness."

14

Farel knew at once what he was up against. One look at Alec Bruno's grim face told him the CIA presentation had been very effective. Of course it must have helped to bring the news everyone wanted to hear. Unlike him. Not only was he bringing bad news, but he was an outsider challenging all kinds of insider loyalties—Washington was as incestuous as a primitive village; the federal government was like a vast private club. His audience was likely to be hostile.

He entered, however, as if he were sure of being accepted, exuding vigorous self-confidence. Putting his bulging brief-case on the table in front of him, he sat down facing the president and then glanced around at the other familiar Washington faces with an amiable smile, showing none of Dober's respect for status, rank, power. He had files on them all, knew their backgrounds—not the personal gossip, but the extent of their professional experience, their strengths and their weaknesses. The director of Central Intelligence came from the military, a lanky forceful man who upgraded front-line agents and downgraded analysis; the secretary of state, wrinkled and nervous, was originally from the academic world and still had a basic intellectual discipline . . . He knew them all, but that wasn't the reason for his confidence. Much as he distrusted the judgment of politicians, Farel was sure they would be won round by his assembly of facts, the sheer power of his logic. He was an incorrigible optimist.

"Mr. Farel," said the president with a friendly smile—he'd been warned Farel could be difficult—"We're very grateful for your attendance here today. As I believe you know, we have to decide between conflicting predictions. We've already received Mr. Bruno's account of his meeting with you, but it'll help us greatly to hear directly from you how you reached your conclusion, and also to have you available here for questioning."

"I'm glad to oblige, Mr. President," Farel replied. "I wish to do all I can to make sure the federal government reaches the correct decision. I've completed my analysis and it should be sufficient to give you the results of it. I'm in no way appearing here as a salesman trying to sell you my point of view over that of the Central Intelligence Agency. I believe the facts will speak for themselves." He looked quizzically at his stony-faced audience. "But you must listen objectively. You must be completely open-minded. Don't decide until I have finished tracing the evidence for you . . ."

Even while he was talking, Farel was assessing the strength of the opposition. The CIA was naturally against him from the start. A lot more depended on the success of their case than just influencing the president's Polish policy. There had been a move to try to split up the CIA and take away its clandestine operations and greatly reduce its powers —this was backed by the State Department—and so the conflict over Poland also became an arena for a much wider disagreement. The Defense Intelligence Agency was on the CIA's side, and therefore the Pentagon representatives, including the influential chairman of the Joint Chiefs, would all be against him. It was a strong team. Farel wondered how much he could rely on the secretary of state, his official backer, against this formidable opposition. Probably not much, he thought, if the secretary of state found he had no allies and the CIA was obviously going to win. He was a vague liberal dove with an academic and legal background, who'd had a safe life at the top among the big corporations, untried in political in-fighting; he'd probably concede early without a real fight in order not to lose too much prestige with the president. Bruno's gloomy attitude no doubt reflected his.

Farel decided his best bet was the president himself. Under some previous presidents, the director of Central Intelligence or the secretary of state, whoever was dominant at the time, would have heard the evidence and then merely presented the president with a recommendation, which was, in effect, a decision. But this president was determined to be the boss as far as possible, to master all the conflicting intelligence groups, and therefore he couldn't afford to take sides—or short cuts. He had to consider the evidence himself. Reaching the right decision in this case might also be important to his own survival in the election. But to convince the president to accept bad news obviously required great persuasion.

"I'd like to preface my analysis with a reference to recent Soviet statements about the importance of Poland to the Soviet Union's overall security on its European flank . . ." It wasn't strictly part of his analysis, but it was fair to use the statements as a preface. He rattled off very accurately long quotations from various Soviet leaders over the last twelve months. The statements were remarkably alike even in the phrases used, as if the Soviet leaders all had the same speech writer. "Poland, you see," Farel summed up, "is not a buffer to be lightly thrown away. The Soviet Union still values it greatly as part of its frontier with Western Europe."

The director of Central Intelligence leaned forward. "You're suggesting that this proves the Soviet Union wouldn't under any circumstances risk allowing the Polish government to have more independence, to become more liberalized?"

127

"I'm suggesting nothing," Farel replied politely, "except that we should bear these statements in mind."

"I could quote an equal number of statements by Soviet leaders on the value of détente and relaxing restrictions," the director said. "Their official statements mean little."

"On the surface, perhaps," Farel said. "But underneath they are trying to put something over. That is what we analysts have to look for."

"What you have to find is the nitty-gritty under all the official garbage," said the director, "and that's precisely what we've found here—a Soviet source that came across with the truth!" The director glanced round at the others with a pleased expression; one or two nodded in agreement.

"I've no wish to debate you," Farel said impatiently. "You missed the point of what I told the president. I'm not trying to sell my conclusion to this meeting. I'm merely going to describe the evidence and the course of my analysis. What this meeting does with it is the president's business, not my responsibility. I'm a kremlinologist, not a politician."

"We understand that," the president said briskly, intent on keeping the peace. "Please continue, Mr. Farel."

"Certainly, Mr. President, but I'd be grateful if any further questions could be kept until I've run through all the evidence."

Farel began to unpack his briefcase. He took his time. He brought out files, clippings, newspapers, magazines, and journals, and placed them in a neat pile in front of him. All eyes were on the pile as if he were a magician about to produce a rabbit. Some of the intelligence people there still thought in terms of cloak-and-dagger melodrama, Farel thought. They weren't yet mature enough to appreciate the classical detachment of analysis. There would be no rabbits out of hats (or briefcases) from him, but nevertheless he would bend their minds by the sheer weight of his argument

128

—in the end they would all reach the same conclusion he had.

He began slowly by summarizing the evidence that led him to predict the Polish uprising, the increasing social exchanges between factories he discovered, and other similarities to the other periods of worker uprisings in 1956 and 1970. "As you know, the prediction proved to be correct," he said quietly, "and so then the question to be answered became: What was the Soviet Union going to do about it? Although the Soviet leadership, as I've pointed out, is on record as to Poland's continued importance to Soviet security, I didn't let this influence my search for an answer. I merely increased the range and intensity of my inquiries, of my reading through current Soviet and East European publications. For several days the question remained unanswered. I was completely open-minded. Then, gentlemen, I found . . ." Ah, yes, let them have their rabbit. ". . . this!" And with a dramatic gesture, he held up a small, badly printed newspaper.

"I received this obscure rural social publication from an old Estonian friend who paid a visit to Georgia—Soviet Georgia, of course, not our state." Farel allowed himself a slight smile as he opened the newspaper to an inside page and pointed to a paragraph ringed in red. They had probably read about it already in Bruno's report, but he intended to woo them himself. "You know what this paragraph says? It reports that a soldier's marriage has been postponed because his leave has been cancelled! That was my first clue, Mr. President."

He passed the newspaper across to the president, who glanced at it quickly and then handed it on down the table. Farel wondered how many of them could read Russian and the other Soviet languages.

He next took a cheap magazine from the pile and

opened it at the sports section, where a paragraph was circled in red at the bottom of the page. "Here is a report that a football game between an army unit and a local team has been cancelled. Very well! Now I began to sense a trend."

He passed the magazine to the president and next took a small, slim journal from the pile. That, too, was handed to the president. Then another newspaper . . . then a magazine . . . soon a line of about twenty publications was moving around the table as Farel commented with boyish enthusiasm. "I quickly found many more examples of army leaves being cancelled, events involving the army being postponed, all in these very obscure local publications—so obscure and local that Soviet censorship might well miss them or think them safely out of range of Western kremlinology. But," he added proudly, "they were mistaken."

He paused; no one made a sound, all eyes were on him. Assured he still held his audience, he went on to marshal yet more references and cross-references. He made the work seem so simple and matter-of-fact that only a fellow analyst like Bruno, who had failed to find the obscure data with a team of helpers and whole warehouses of information, could fully appreciate Farel's brilliance and the range of his industry. Farel had an unerring instinct for selecting which clues to pursue—clues that were sometimes never even uncovered in the government's prodigious flow of signals and photo reconnaissance data picked up by the new spy satellites and electronic monitoring devices.

At last Farel sat back.

"I must apologize, Mr. President," he said, "for boring you with such a tedious presentation, but analysis essentially consists of the laborious assembling of a multitude of small facts that together provide a complete answer. It's the technique of the jigsaw, fitting the pieces together—interesting to do, dull to watch. I wouldn't have submitted you to it in such detail if my analysis hadn't been challenged. I trust that I have now proved my conclusion."

The President seemed to nod, very serious, and was about to reply when the director of Central Intelligence said quickly, "If you are correct, Mr. Farel, why hasn't the Soviet army gone back into Poland already? The quicker they move, the easier it'll be to crush the revolt. Each day they wait the Polish workers' resistance will harden and become better organized. So far there is no visible evidence at all to back your contention. Aerial reconnaissance has spotted no mass army movements. The satellites—the same—nothing!"

Farel thoughtfully straightened his pile of evidence and then said slowly, "The lack of aerial data doesn't worry me —the Soviet Union is as clever as we are at camouflaging what they're doing. I'd expect a quicker warning from ground intelligence." He glanced at the secretary of defense and the chairman of the Joint Chiefs. "I'm sure you have inside contacts in the Soviet army, or at least close-range electronic coverage, gentlemen. You'll know when they cross the frontier."

"But why haven't they done so already?" pressed the director.

Farel said impatiently, "You know as well as I do their curious ignorance and paranoia concerning our presidential election process. They seem to think we're capable of doing anything during a presidential election campaign. I can quote you, as I'm sure Mr. Bruno can, a dozen references from Soviet leaders and Soviet publications about their fears arising from the closeness of the presidential race this year." He looked directly at the president. "I deal in facts, not in speculations, but I think they have probably delayed crushing the Polish revolt because they fear that if they did so in the last week of a very close presidential race here, you, Mr. President, might be driven into some reckless adventure to help you to win. I conclude they will go back

131

into Poland this coming week after our election is over and our—your—reaction will be more pragmatic, more reasonable."

"A very interesting theory," said the director. "But what evidence is there that isn't merely circumstantial or coincidental? Is it really sufficient to stand against the report of a Soviet informant who says the Soviet Union has definitely decided to stay out?"

"To me," Farel said calmly, "an informant is just one source of evidence, and that isn't enough. He may be right, he may be wrong. As an analyst, I need many such pieces of evidence from different sources before I feel able to reach a conclusion."

"This wasn't a paragraph in an obscure journal, Mr. Farel. This was a senior Soviet embassy official who passed a polygraph test and was killed for passing on the information to us."

"I read of his death," Farel said.

"Did you notice the official Soviet comment?"

"I did."

"Didn't you think it strange that, if the Soviet army intends to crush the workers, an attempt wasn't made to blame them for the murder?"

"I must admit their 'no comment' mystified me. I don't know what the explanation is. There's something behind it I don't understand—yet."

"Isn't it more in keeping with a hands-off policy, a decision to stay out?"

"Perhaps—if there wasn't so much evidence pointing the other way."

"Circumstantial evidence."

Farel said impatiently, "I know a young man who is being held for a murder on far less evidence than I have given you regarding the Soviet Union's plans."

"Did the young man take a polygraph test, Mr. Farel?"

132

"The polygraph isn't a one hundred percent sure method of detecting lies."

The president glanced at his watch. "If nobody has any more questions . . ." The others took the hint and no one spoke. "Well, then, I think we should let Mr. Farel go. We've kept him long enough. Thank you very much, sir, for your invaluable assistance."

They shook hands.

Farel began to load his briefcase. It was impossible to read the mood of the meeting, but he was confident they had understood his analysis. The director of Central Intelligence went over to whisper to the president. Pete Baldwin leaned forward to listen—he was from the president's home town, had been in naval intelligence; he was supposed to be the president's special assistant on national security affairs, but he was little more than a messenger and a sounding board for the president, not an adviser capable of standing up to the other intelligence experts. The president was on his own in making his decision.

On his way out, Farel was stopped by a grave-faced secretary of state, who shook his hand but didn't say anything. Farel nodded and passed on. The secretary hadn't been much help against the opposition. Bruno whispered, "Wait outside for me."

He waited in the side office for nearly an hour. He listened to two Secret Servicemen talk about their wives. Then the door suddenly opened and there was a rush of people. Bruno was one of the last out. He came in the side office and looked at Farel and slowly shook his head.

Farel couldn't believe it. "Are they crazy?" he cried, standing up. For a moment he was lost in a rare wave of emotion, then he controlled himself. "They're wrong," he said quietly. "They're making a big mistake, Bruno. Wait and see . . ."

133

15

Dober was treated like a winner at the two-story stucco building near the Library of Congress. CIA executives he'd never met clapped him on the back and called him Frank, and even the secretaries gave him wide, friendly smiles as he waited for the director to return from the White House.

"Sorry to keep you waiting, Frank," the director said jovially when at last he came striding in. "It's been a long day for all of us, but it was worth it."

He led Dober through the restricted area, past the electronic gear analyzing Soviet radar signals, and into his ornate office. A guard carefully closed the door behind them.

"The president's leaving to hit the campaign trail again. He wanted my advice about how to handle Poland in his speeches," the director confided, offering Dober an expensive cigar, relaxing as if they were teammates in the winners' locker room. "He's got a major address, to be covered by all the media, coming up tomorrow in Michigan, where a lot of Polish immigrants have settled. His advance men are there already arranging for a big crowd that'll look good on TV. I practically told him what to say."

The director described how "very flattering" the president had been in talking about the Agency. "He was full of praise of our excellent front-line organization and our penetration of the Soviet embassy. He was very impressed by your testimony, Frank. You deserve a vacation with your family. Take a couple of weeks off. Give that wound time to heal."

He'd been chewing on a cigar, now he lit it and puffed vigorously. The cloud of smoke tickled Dober's sinuses. "Your cover's blown in Warsaw, Frank, so join the Berlin station until the situation in Poland quiets down. You'll be valuable there as a coordinator of the Polish coverage, and you can always make a brief trip across the border with the help of the Polish underground if you have to. And then, Frank, I want you to return to Washington to work with Mervyn Podz on overall Soviet long-range analysis. Your experience," the director added with a warm smile, "will be invaluable in preventing Podz from becoming too theoretical and artificial like Farel and those other chairbound types."

It was a big promotion and explained why the director had wanted to see him alone, without Hinds. Dober was pleased. He was growing tired of front-line station work in spite of the liberal expense allowance. Maybe he was getting too old for it and belonged behind a desk in Washington, out of the cold. His wife'd be happier there, and the kids'd have a chance to get to know their own country.

Before he left for Berlin, he met Hinds in a bar downtown. It was the kind of noisy pickup bar that Hinds would like. Hinds was going to Madrid as station chief. It was a promotion, too, and Hinds was very cocky, very full of himself, and Dober felt the old dislike for the small, hairy man coming back.

"They had to give us something. We've saved the Agency's neck. Back in favor at the White House, no more talk of splitting it up. We've put the director back in the saddle. I rubbed it in when I was talking to him. I told him about that hellish drive through the Warsaw back streets, the Russians on our tail, you wounded and almost out of action. We barely made it that time, old buddy. The Poles were so slow, so amateurish at the game. I felt like kicking their ass . . ."

135

It was a colorful ego trip, and it irritated Dober, made him uncomfortable, uneasy—boasting like that was tempting fate. He left early for the airport to get away from Hinds. Hinds stayed behind in the bar. His inflated ego that night demanded a woman, any woman. She'd be like a lump of meat thrown to an animal in the zoo, Dober thought gloomily.

His earlier good mood had vanished, thanks to Hinds, and he couldn't shake off a depressed feeling all the way across the Atlantic. He picked at the assembly-line frozen food, he drank some more Scotch, he tried to sleep—the plane was half empty; he had a row to himself—but his mood wouldn't change. The vitamin and energy shots were wearing off. He wondered what his wife had been doing.

He was met at the airport by the Berlin deputy chief, a quiet, efficient, youngish man named Mills he knew slightly —the director had arranged for the red-carpet treatment. On the way into the city in Mills's Cadillac, he inquired about the latest Polish news. The government was meeting with the workers' leaders; everyone was waiting to find out what kind of agreement they would reach. Dober felt strangely relieved, and he at last began to regain some of his earlier cheerfulness. The Polish government wouldn't be doing that if there was any chance of the Soviet army coming back. There was no doubt Ivan was right. Rest in peace, my playboy friend.

Dober's thoughts turned happily to his reunion with his wife and kids. He had discarded the sling and, with his arm only slightly bandaged, he could wear his jacket. Clara wouldn't know he'd been wounded until he undressed for bed . . .

They were working late at the news magazine on the last issue before the election. The presidential candidates were now on the cover, but there was a long special report on

136

Poland inside that had kept Frances Cernik busy all evening. Their Warsaw bureau had sent two long additions very late. The Catholic cardinal, who had already spoken out against police brutality, had delivered a stirring sermon in St. John's Cathedral in favor of the workers. Soon after, the Polish government conceded to worker demands and replaced some of its hard-line ministers with more liberal, pro-worker political leaders; if that didn't satisfy the workers, the next step would probably be the fall of the government unless the Soviet Union stepped in. And now approaching the deadline, the Russians still hadn't made a move.

Midnight came and went, and finally her boss decided they'd have to go with what they'd got. He sat back and took out a bottle of Scotch and poured them both a big drink. He had a liquor problem, but he was pretty good about not starting to drink until the deadline was passed. She abandoned her desk, crowded with files, clippings and proofs, and relaxed in his office facing the fine panoramic view of downtown, a bigger status symbol at the magazine than even the thick green wall-to-wall carpet. The lights were out in most of the downtown buildings now—it was too late even for the cleaning women. At least the magazine sent you home in a cab after midnight.

"We could've finished much earlier," she said yawning, plastic glass in hand, "if only Warsaw'd worked out what Russia's up to."

"That damn bureau's so scared of being wrong. The ending we've got is fuzzy, undecided, either-or—no guts." Irritated, he took a long drink. She'd heard him earlier yelling down the long-distance phone at the chief of the Warsaw bureau. For such a mild-mannered man, he could work up a dandy temper. He refilled his glass. She promised herself to be out of there before he started reminiscing about the good old days as a war correspondent in Korea and Vietnam, a sure sign he was plastered. He'd probably spend the night on the office couch. The late closing gave him a great excuse to go on drinking.

The outside phone buzzed. He was slow to pick it up, assuming it was his wife checking up on him. Then, as he listened, his chubby face lost its relaxed look and grew serious, the liquor forgotten. "Okay," he said at last. "We've passed the deadline, but we'll reopen the page. This is too good to miss. Can you put it over right away? . . . That's good."

He banged down the receiver, pushed away his glass, and reached for a pad and pencil. "Sorry, Fran, we relaxed a little too soon, but we've got a real ending after all." She watched him writing a new headline as he talked. "The president's giving a news conference. Washington's decided the Soviet Union's staying out. The Warsaw bureau'll be happy. We can be definite at Washington's expense. One of the bureau's CIA buddies leaked it, probably on the director's instructions—it's good for the CIA's image."

He picked up the interoffice phone and then replaced it. "On second thoughts, a personal appearance downstairs might be better. They'll be mad as hell." A golf club leaning against the wall attracted his attention. He swung it lightly and lifted a ball of paper on the floor toward the window. "Hole in one," he said with satisfaction and hurried out. He was still a working pro—the liquor hadn't torn him down yet.

Peace again. She'd be needed later to check the story and then the proof, but there was plenty of time—they'd probably be there until dawn now. She decided to keep busy doing her expenses while she was waiting, while he was out of the office and she could consult his day book. She'd been careless about keeping her diary up-to-date; maybe his day book would jog her memory.

The last item in her diary was her appointment with Ur-

138

sula the day that Ursula was killed. Who was it she'd interviewed earlier that day to check a story? She'd forgotten to note it. She turned to that day in his book. A line was crossed out. She held the page up to the light and saw that he'd had an appointment with Ursula that day—the day she was killed. For some reason it came as a shock.

She remembered how he'd refused to talk to Leo Farel's assistant. She'd blamed his damn paranoia, his drinking—he took himself too seriously sometimes, was always wanting to hide behind his lawyer—but maybe he did have something to hide.

She couldn't read the time of the appointment, just Ursula's name. Maybe it had been that evening, though Ursula had seemed in no hurry when they met earlier for a cocktail. Maybe his wife had found out . . . maybe he'd wanted to end it . . . She remembered his hand gripping the golf club, the long strong fingers around the shaft . . . Oh, don't be crazy, she told herself. He's too weak, you know he is . . .

She'd just finished adding up her expenses when he returned. She was owed ninety-eight bucks; no wonder she was short this week.

He slapped the story down on her desk. "It's worth waiting for, Fran."

She began carefully to read through it. "I hope I won't need those files I loaned Ursula. The precinct promised to release them, but they haven't arrived yet." She added casually, "Did Ursula ever mention the files to you?"

"Why do you ask?"

She gave him an innocent look. "I thought maybe you saw her after I gave them to her and she mentioned them. Maybe that last day—"

"Fran, my lawyer advised me not to discuss it with anyone."

"I'm not anyone."

"We-ll . . . yes, I was going to see her that last day. At her

139

place. But she phoned me to cancel it. Why I don't know. She didn't give any reason. She never did give any reason. Fran"—he sat on the edge of the desk, looking down at her —"Ursula was a friend of yours. You saw her differently. You're a woman. You'd have to be a man to see the Ursula I saw. She could be a real bitch. She even threatened to tell my wife. She had some idea we should get married. My God, if you knew her the way I did—she was real sick, and I mean sick!"

He got up hurriedly, as if he'd said too much. "We better get out the story, Fran, and talk about this later." He disappeared inside his office, and she soon heard the rattle of ice cubes.

There wouldn't be any "later"—he'd be too plastered. She settled down to check the story, feeling very disturbed.

The landlord was a small, white-haired man with a Florida tan and large melancholy eyes, who talked as if the current wave of inflation had been created especially to ruin him. If any tenant tackled him directly about essential repairs, he made wild promises just to get away. The promises were never kept and he left the old superintendent to deal with complaints. He was secretly trying to sell the house and had no intention of spending any more money on it. Let the next landlord spend his money.

Mrs. Charles, who had been trying to get a faulty radiator repaired for weeks, found him talking to the old super outside Ursula Rogal's apartment. The rent was up at the end of the week, and the landlord was beginning to get worried about his money. "The police will have to remove her belongings," he was telling the superintendent, "or you'll have to dump them on the sidewalk for the garbage men. She left no will, and they're trying to get in touch with her relatives in Poland. But in the meantime I can't possibly afford to lose any rent on the apartment, not with inflation steadily bank-

140

rupting me. Don't breathe a word about the murder to any prospective tenants. It might put them off, you understand."

"There's going to be another murder in this house unless you do something about my radiator," Mrs. Charles cried, coming up behind the landlord.

He glanced round, startled.

"My plants are going to be suffocated," she said.

He realized he was cornered; his large melancholy eyes pleaded for sympathy. "These workmen are so unreliable."

"You told me that last month."

"Trust me. We're getting, ah, a new piece from the factory," he said smoothly. "They were out of stock. Next Monday . . ."

"I'll wait until then, but no longer." Now if he'd been murdered, she could have understood it. Everyone in the house would have been a suspect.

"If you want to wait," he said with a sudden inspiration, "you could move into this empty apartment. The rent's the same and the radiator works perfectly."

"And Ursula Rogal was murdered there. No thanks."

Al Rivera was coming down the stairs in a smart, closely fitting dark suit. "Is that apartment really available?" he asked cheerfully.

"The rent's paid up until the end of the week," the landlord said carefully. "It will then be available, up for grabs."

"I'd like to take it," Rivera said. "It's in better shape than mine and it's bigger. I've been upstairs over a year. I'd welcome a change."

"You don't mind about the murder?" asked Mrs. Charles.

"I don't believe in ghosts."

Rivera seemed eager; the others stared strangely at him, even the landlord.

Basketball practice was just ending when Perry saw the priest enter the school gymnasium and stand at the back, watching. There was a rush down the court, a struggle under the net, a fumbled ball, and then Perry blew his whistle. As the players rushed noisily and sweatily to the changing rooms, Perry walked over to the priest. He looked familiar. What did he want?

Father Joyce introduced himself. "I read in the *News* that your student has been formally charged. I came to see if there's anything I can do to help."

"He has a lawyer," Perry said. "There's not much more that can be done."

"You sound almost . . . Pardon me, but you sound as if you think he's guilty."

Perry pulled out a handkerchief and mopped his face. It gave him time to think. Why had the priest come to him? He was only Willie's coach, not his father.

"I think Willie could have done it if he'd been forced into a situation. . . . Father Joyce, I understand that you knew Miss Rogal. I don't want to offend you. She was not . . . she wasn't my favorite colleague. In fact, I didn't like her."

Father Joyce nodded as if he understood. "You don't offend me. I hardly knew her. But anyway our obligation now is to the living. As the boy's coach, you must be very close to him. That's why I've come to you . . ."

The priest suddenly seemed much more Irish than American—much more foreign. How long had he been in the States? Perry felt embarrassed. Perhaps he should have done more to help Willie.

"What were you thinking of?"

"I've so little experience of legal procedures . . ."

"The trial will have to take its course now. He's got a lawyer, and Leo Farel is taking an interest in the case—he's an influential man, I understand. He can do much more than someone like me. The only other thing that would help Willie would be if the real killer was caught."

"But if he did it—under provocation, I mean—then . . ."

142

"Then, Father, there's not much you or I or Leo Farel or anybody else can do."

The priest nodded thoughtfully.

"Thank you, Mr. Perry. Sorry to have bothered you."

"No bother. Good of you to come."

Perry began to relax as the priest walked away across the basketball court. He'd had the impression the priest was holding back something—something that he was going to bring out as a sudden shocker—and Perry had tensed up waiting for it. There's nothing he can accuse me of, Perry thought, slowly following the priest out of the gymnasium. But still Father Joyce had made him feel guilty.

So much of research was checking trivial details. Sometimes it paid off. The files Ursula Rogal had borrowed from the magazine worried Henrik, and so he phoned Frances Cernik to find out more about them. His call came at the right time. The police had returned the files, and she had just checked through them. She was very chatty and friendly.

"It's very strange," she said, "but one set of clippings is missing. I checked with the police. They haven't kept them and they're not in Ursula's apartment. They're definitely missing. When I've got the time, I'll have to trace them and get a duplicate set made."

"What did they refer to?"

"Auschwitz, the worst of the camps."

"Was that where her father was killed?"

"No, he died in Lyuboml, but she and her mother were there for a short time. In fact, I think her mother died there."

"Maybe the clippings just fell out."

"Then they would have been found in the apartment. No, I told her to take good care of them, and Ursula was very practical. It's very strange."

16

Farel had arrived back from Washington looking pale, drawn, unsmiling. "Maximum depression," said Virgie in telling Henrik about it. She knew all her father's moods, but this worried even her. Farel had told her he didn't want any dinner, he was going to work all night. Before she went to bed, he said, he'd be grateful if she'd leave him a plate of sandwiches and a glass of milk outside the Ivory Tower, in case he was hungry later. He was distantly polite, "very abstract," his mind elsewhere. She tried to tell him about Willie, but he said impatiently, "Later, Virgie, later." That was the last she'd seen of him. "I don't know what happened in Washington," she told Henrik, frowning, very concerned, "but it must have been something pretty bad. Leo looked really grim."

Henrik smiled sympathetically at her. Sometimes Farel forgot she was still a child and treated her like a grown woman. Already she was too serious for her age, too shy, too studious. She needed to laugh more! To sing! To be happy! Like the children he remembered in Estonia when he was a boy! The only person who really made her laugh was Willie —he taught her the latest songs, the things that young people her age were interested in. She missed another woman in the house, Henrik thought. If there were someone to help her spend more time on her appearance and her clothes, she could look really pretty . . . Farel was still young and present-able enough to get married again, but what American woman today would accept being second best to his work? Ah, Henrik told himself, geniuses shouldn't get married and have children.

"Don't worry," he told her, "I'll go and see what the problem is."

He mounted the stairs with a strong sense of duty, know-ing the kind of scene he would find and not looking forward to it.

The usually orderly Ivory Tower was a mess. Newspapers and magazines littered the floor. Farel was bowed over an immense pile of clippings. When he looked up, his eyes were bloodshot and he needed a shave.

"Hello, Henrik. Is it that time already?"

Farel yawned and stretched. In front of him on the desk were the latest Foreign Broadcast Information Service daily reports on Eastern Europe and the Soviet Union. He'd marked a report from the "Warsaw Domestic Service" in Polish—something about Soviet shipments—Henrik couldn't see more than the heading. Farel patted the pile in front of him, the result of his obsessive night's search. "I've been through everything that's come in over the last two days. I've found a dozen pieces of evidence confirming my analysis and not a damn whisper against. I've got to tell Bruno. The president must reconsider. The sheer weight of evidence is overwhelming."

Henrik saw the light then. "You mean," he said, aston-ished, "Washington doesn't accept your analysis?"

Farel sighed. "The CIA's come up with some Soviet spy who claims the opposite. You know how impressed they always are by such front-line romantic twaddle. But this time they can't get away with it. The evidence is too great. Every item supports my conclusion. Although not hard evidence, even some general reports in the FBI's summaries, such as

145

the announcement here of further Soviet grain shipments to Poland, only make real sense if my analysis is accepted."

"But, you say, Washington's already rejected it?"

"Temporarily, Henrik. That's why I spent all night turning up yet more evidence. If really contrary facts were going to show up, now was the time for them. But I've found none —none at all! Washington will have to accept it now."

He phoned Bruno at the State Department. Bruno didn't sound too pleased to hear from him.

"Farel, the matter's settled," he said coldly, but Farel interrupted enthusiastically. "Now don't give me your bureaucratic voice, Bruno. I've discovered new evidence and you must present it to the president immediately." Bruno tried to say something, but Farel swept on, listing each new piece of evidence—source, summary, meaning—while Henrik thought about the cost of the call. Farel should have phoned collect, except that the State Department might not have accepted the call.

At last he was finished. "Well, what do you say to that, Bruno?" he asked confidently.

There was a pause and then Bruno, sounding very distant, said wearily, "Impressive, but you don't seem to realize, Farel, the case is closed. The decision has been made."

"Reopen the case, unmake the decision!"

"Impossible, Farel. While we're talking here, the president is already making a speech in Michigan congratulating the Soviet Union for staying out of it. He's committed himself —and the country. Turn your TV on. You'll see him for yourself. I'm sorry, but there's nothing more we can do."

It was Farel's turn to be silent.

"Farel, are you there?"

"Yes . . ." He clenched his teeth. "The election's only two days off, Bruno, and then the Russians will make their move. You'll hear about it first from aerial reconnaissance or your

146

border observers. Give me a call when you get the news—the news proving I'm right."

Bruno seemed to think that was amusing and they ended the exchange rather coldly.

"They're determined to make fools of themselves," Farel told Henrik gloomily. "All we can do now is wait . . ."

They watched the President on TV. He came on very strongly: forthright, serious-faced, earnest, gesturing vigorously. He conveyed the impression that the United States had persuaded the Soviet Union to stay out. "We're reaping the benefits of being strong. We've moved a step nearer truly peaceful coexistence on this planet. And meanwhile"—the president eyed the large signs of the Polish immigrants prominently displayed at the front of the enthusiastic crowd in Michigan—"our Polish friends can relax and concentrate on the tasks ahead without interference. . . ."

It was an effective campaign speech, well timed; with election day two days off, it just had time to influence the voters.

Farel sat watching, expressionless. Henrik could see no sign of what he must be feeling. But Leo was a realist: he could accept bad news.

Virgie and Willie's grandmother, accompanied by a black youth about Willie's age, came in toward the end.

They listened until the president finished and then Virgie said, "But I thought, Leo, you told me they were going back in."

"They will."

"Then the president—"

"—is wrong."

"Oh, Leo!" She kissed him impulsively. Then she gave him a sly look. "Now you'll have plenty of time to help Willie."

"Virgie, you ought to see my desk. It's piled high with all the things that are waiting for me to have some time: the

147

latest developments in Sino-Soviet relations—I'm way behind there and have to catch up—then there are the latest Soviet moves in the Middle East and Africa—"

"Oh, Leo!"

"—and, of course," he conceded quickly, "there's Willie, too."

"Frankie here," Virgie said, introducing the black youth sitting next to her, "is a friend of Willie's. He's got something to tell you, Leo." As the youth looked shyly at his feet, she encouraged him, "Go ahead, Frankie. Tell Leo."

"Okay." Frankie leaned forward, looking earnestly at Farel. "I work at the supermarket, Mr. Farel, taking deliveries. The day before she—Miss Rogal—was murdered, I took her groceries round to her." He now had Farel's full attention. "She was on the phone when I got there. She went on talking low while I was unloading the box in the kitchen. She was having some kind of an argument. I heard her saying, 'Yes, I'm going to tell unless . . .' "

"Unless what?" Farel said.

"She didn't say."

"Did you hear her say anything else?"

"No, then I was ready to go."

"But it sounded like a threat?"

"Sure."

"Have you told the police?"

"No, all they'd do is say it was Willie. But it wasn't one of her students, it was somebody older. I could tell the way she was talking to them. But they'd say it was Willie."

"Sometimes when you get an idea in your head," Farel said thoughtfully, "it's hard to see any other point of view."

"I guess so," Frankie said.

"Willie's feeling very depressed," Virgie said.

"I bet he is." Farel looked sympathetically across at Willie's grandmother, who was patting Frankie's knee approvingly.

148

"He's had nothing but bad news. The police have formally charged him. Haven't you any good news for him, Leo?"

"Not yet, Virgie. Remember, I'm only just back from Washington and I was working all night."

"I know, but what now, Leo?"

"I've prepared a report," Henrik said helpfully. "And we've received a preliminary report from Warsaw from Stanislaw Grotow in today's mail. I haven't yet had a chance to read it."

"Good," Farel said briskly, welcoming the chance to relax his mind on this trivial murder case after the frustrations of Washington. "I'll read those reports first and then I'll go through our complete file on the case—everything! A definite pattern should emerge leading to the right person. Then perhaps, Virgie, I'll have some news for Willie, good or bad."

"It'll be good," she said.

The report from Warsaw was incomplete. Grotow was in bed with influenza; he'd only been able to speak to Ursula Rogal's relatives by phone. He promised a second report in a few days when he was well enough to visit them. Grotow was a hypochondriac—he was always in bed with something —but Farel wondered if this was a diplomatic illness to keep him out of trouble during the present uprising. He'd had flu in 1970, too.

"Her remaining relatives in Warsaw are her father's brother and sister, both unmarried," Grotow wrote in Polish. As he read, Farel remembered Grotow as he'd last seen him two years ago, sitting up in bed in an elegant red robe, worrying about the drafts from the door and window. "They live together in a rather dreary prefabricated apartment block in the Bielany District—I know the area well because I have friends who live there, too. The sister did all the talking to me on the phone and seemed a garrulous but

149

reliable person. I'll check this impression when I meet her within the next few days.

"She told me that Ursula Rogal was born in Lyuboml, which, as you'll know, Mr. Farel, is a very small, undistinguished border town. Her father, whose name was Rogalski and who worked in a brick factory there, was killed in 1943 when members of the Ukrainian militia, an enforcement arm of the Nazi SS, mistook him for a Jew. He was made to dig a pit and then stand over it while a lieutenant named Anatole Bach shot him in the back of the head. You'll no doubt recall that several thousand Polish Jews were killed in Lyuboml in the early nineteen-forties.

"Ursula Rogalski—as she was then—and her mother were taken to a prison camp about ten kilometers away, and then later they were transferred to Auschwitz. The Nazis never admitted making a mistake and the Rogalskis were treated as Jews. Her mother died in Auschwitz, but Ursula Rogalski survived—she was there only a short time and one of the guards took a fancy to her. By then her relatives I'm in touch with had moved from Lyuboml to Warsaw, and when Auschwitz was liberated, she went to live with them. They found her much changed. She'd been a happy, playful child, but now she was a withdrawn, irritable girl, very thin and sickly, with very little interest in other people. They weren't sorry when she won a travelling scholarship and decided to study in France.

"After graduation, Ursula Rogalski went to work for the United States army, and in 1952 she emigrated to the U.S.A. Her relatives had no more news of her for fifteen years, and then she came back for a month's visit. They were her only living relatives and she greeted them very warmly, but they were embarrassed to find that she was a complete stranger to them—they couldn't recognize her. In place of the withdrawn, sullen teenager they remembered was an attractive, sophisticated, outgoing American woman. They had to get

150

to know her all over again. They discovered she was still very much interested in Poland and was a little ashamed she had shortened the family name of Rogalski to Rogal in America —'The Americans found our name rather hard to pronounce,' she explained. [Ah, Farel thought, she ought to have tried pronouncing my name in Estonian! I had to drop several vowels in America!] She remembered very clearly all the events surrounding her father's death and, on this visit, she employed a private detective in Warsaw to try to find out what had happened to her father's killer, Lieutenant Anatole Bach, who was notorious for his cruelty in the Lyuboml area. Her dream was to trace him and get him extradited back to Poland to be tried and punished. This surprised her old relatives because, to them, the tragedy was now part of the distant past—it was the Soviet occupation that obsessed them. They attributed her obsession to the Auschwitz experience and to the protected life she had lived in America since then. Although they found her a little too aggressive and self-opinionated by the behavior standards of Polish women, they gradually warmed to her and tried to persuade her to go back to Catholicism, which she had given up since leaving Poland. But they had no luck there. She had no interest in religion, she told them. The only argument they had during her visit was over religion. She claimed the Vatican could have done much more against Hitler than it did, and they told her she was mistaken, and they quoted examples of priests who had stood up against the Nazis in Poland, just as similar priests were standing up against the Communists today—not that they linked the Communists and the Nazis together! They wonder now whether her aggressive nature led to her violent death.

"After this visit, she wrote regularly to them and sent them gifts. She told them in detail about her hunt for Lieutenant Bach, as if they were as obsessed as she was. The Warsaw detective had found out that Bach had emigrated to

151

North or South America under another name. For a time, she employed a detective agency in New York, but with no results. In a recent letter, she reported that she'd been in touch with a specialist in Nazi hunting in the U.S.A. She was still obsessed with revenge—her old relatives considered it a reflection of her lack of religion! In the same recent letter, she also wrote that she might be getting married.

"At the start of our recent troubles, she phoned them once to find out if they were all right. She said she was really worried about them—apparently the gravity of the situation here had been exaggerated by the Western press. We Poles are perfectly capable of dealing with our own problems! But her old relatives were touched by her expensive, long-distance phone call, and they are greatly distressed by her murder. They would like to know if she made a will.

"This is about all I discovered on the phone. I found it difficult to keep the talkative woman to the point. But no doubt I'll discover more when I meet them. Thank you for the clippings about the murder. I'll show them to her relatives."

Farel handed the report back to Henrik for filing.

"It doesn't explain why those clippings are missing from the magazine's files. Is there a connection between the missing clippings about Auschwitz and her murder? Did the killer have an interest in them, too, and after killing her, take them away with him? Or destroy them? Did this Lieutenant Bach have any connection with Auschwitz?"

"It is possible," Henrik said.

"But what connection?"

Henrik didn't reply, but waited.

"Ah," Farel said, "we're still dealing with speculations, not facts. Anything is possible. This killer is as good at hiding his motives, his tracks, as the Soviet Union. Henrik, I think your next job better be to trace those clippings in the newspaper library on West Forty-third Street. Miss Cernik can no

152

doubt give you the list of dates and sources. She might even help you to find them. Something in them may explain why they're missing. Also send Grotow a cable thanking him discreetly in code for his report and ask him to go and visit the relatives immediately. Surely his flu, real or imaginary, is over by now. As soon as the Soviet army goes back in, travelling in the capital may be difficult for several days. There may be something more the relatives know, that can be squeezed out of them if Grotow questions them in depth. We need at least the name of that Nazi hunter she consulted. Surely she mentioned it in her letters. If so, tell Grotow to cable us the name."

Henrik got up, notebook in hand.

"Wait. Let me first backtrack over the facts we know. Check me out in case I miss anything."

Henrik sat down again.

"One, the day before the murder Frankie hears her threatening someone she's going to 'tell.' That could be why she was killed—to silence her. But what was it she was going to tell? The police would say she was threatening to tell on Willie, perhaps some fanciful story of attempted rape, and lose him his scholarship if he didn't do what she wanted. It's possible. Everyone has something they might kill for. With Willie, maybe it's that scholarship.

"But Willie's not the only possibility. Take a look at the others. Our magazine editor—she could have threatened to tell his wife. The old super—maybe she threatened to tell the landlord some dirt and lose him his job. Mr. Perry, our basketball coach—maybe he's got a secret. He protests too much about his dislike of her. Or Father Joyce—maybe he's not all he seems. Or your passionate friend, Mr. Rivera. There are numerous possibilities, but few facts."

"Miss Rogal begins to seem not a very nice person," Henrik said.

"Who knows how that period in the concentration camp

153

affected her? She was only ten or eleven when she went in. Some of those young girls were raped or beaten regularly. To go from there to the freedom of America with no restraints, no relatives . . . who knows what the woman became under her public role as the schoolteacher? But that is for artists or judges or psychologists to ponder. That's not my business. I'm after plain simple facts."

He scribbled, "One—what Frankie overheard" on a pad. "All right," he said. "What's fact number two?"

Henrik said, "Willie—"

"That's right. Two, Willie comes by while Ursula Rogal is out, is seen by Mrs. Charles . . . but not by the old super. Did anyone else see him or was Mrs. Charles the only one?"

"She was the only one."

"Curious . . . Well, never mind for now." He made a quick note of it for later. "At the moment we're only listing proven and obviously relevant facts. What's number three? Ursula Rogal has cocktails with Frances Cernik, who has loaned her the files. Four, she sees the old super and enters the building. Five, she sees Mrs. Charles who tells her about Willie. Six, she goes into her apartment and is never seen alive again—"

"Except by the killer."

"Correct. Now we reach the period of the murder. Seven, Mrs. Charles hears Ursula Rogal admit a visitor."

"She swears she heard Willie's voice."

"I think we can discount that as a fact. When you were at the door of Miss Rogal's apartment with the old super, she heard you from roughly where she heard the visitor's voice that day, and, according to your report, she thought you were Mr. Rivera. So much for the accuracy of her identification of Willie! She probably imagined it was Willie because he'd come by earlier and she soon convinced herself she'd actually heard his voice—unless she deliberately lied."

"Perhaps it was Willie."

"Unlikely. Now what is fact number eight?"

154

"Having killed Miss Rogal, the murderer departs."

"Not so fast, Henrik." Farel brooded for a few moments. "We have several facts here and we can't be sure of their exact sequence. Let's list them together, bearing in mind they may not be in the right order.

"The murderer kills and ransacks the rooms in search of something. All that we know for sure is missing are those Auschwitz clippings. Is that what the killer was looking for, or was there something else—several things, perhaps? And what were they? Would they incriminate him?

"But that is mere speculation. Let's proceed with our list:

"The murderer kills, ransacks, and departs.

"The old super goes to the bathroom.

"He also feeds his dog.

"Father Joyce meets the old super outside and enters the building to call on Miss Rogal.

"Mr. Rivera also meets the old super and goes into the building to his apartment on the floor above Miss Rogal's apartment.

"Mrs. Charles, hearing Father Joyce outside, joins him in trying to rouse Miss Rogal.

"The old super comes upstairs and joins Father Joyce and Mrs. Charles.

"He checks Miss Rogal is not with Mr. Rivera.

"The old super, Mr. Rivera, Father Joyce, and Mrs. Charles find the body.

"Now that makes . . . let me see . . . sixteen basic facts in all. The next step is to work out the exact sequence."

"Haven't you missed out one important fact in that period?" Henrik asked.

"No, I don't think so. Some details, yes. What did you have in mind?"

"The murder took place shortly after seven o'clock and a witness saw Willie run away from the block about that time."

"Well, we can call that fact number seventeen if you wish,

155

but I'm inclined to accept Willie's explanation. He came back, saw the police cars, and was afraid of getting involved. It sounds reasonable. But anyway it's a mere detail. It doesn't present us with any problem as to where it comes in the sequence. It clearly comes at the end. I'm mainly interested in what happened up to the murder, not after it."

Farel began to play with the list he'd scribbled down, inserting arrows to change the order several times. Then he sat back, his eyes half closed. Henrik knew that look well. It usually came toward the end of a long period of analysis when Farel let his mind range over the whole field. Usually what happened then was that suddenly the evidence all fell into place and he could see his way through to his conclusion, even though several vital pieces of evidence might be still missing. Such a meditation could take hours, and so Henrik rose quietly, knowing he wouldn't be missed, and set off to do his research at the newspaper library.

Left alone, Farel slowly reread the clippings on the case and then Henrik's two reports and Grotow's letter. Then he returned to his list of basic facts. He was groping for something, some connection between the facts, perhaps, or some elusive memory—he wished his memory were as reliable as his files. Anyway, whatever it was, he couldn't find it. His mind had gone stale. He needed some exercise. He decided to go for a short walk in Central Park.

Downstairs, he heard Virgie and Willie's grandmother in the kitchen as he crept out.

It was a cold, clear November day; the air seemed to wake him up. He walked briskly across the sparse grass, under the bare trees, his mind free to roam. He passed several ball games, several pairs of lovers walking gloved hand in gloved hand, several streams of cyclists on the roadways and paths; the boating lake, shimmering with November sunlight, deserted, soon to be topped with ice, with the skyscrapers far away in the background . . . and he saw and heard none of

156

it. He might have been blind and deaf, with some inner radar guiding him across the park, as his mind busily reordered the facts and suddenly found the connection that had been eluding him.

Of course.

That was the correct sequence.

That was what had happened.

And there was the murderer.

No doubt about it, though there were no facts regarding the motive—yet. They were still to come.

Farel stood still, unaware of where he was, completely preoccupied with his thoughts.

Brakes squealed, voices cursed. He was on his way home in the middle of Central Park West, holding up the traffic. He shook himself, grinned sheepishly, and walked quickly on as if the traffic were to blame.

Virgie and Willie's grandmother were still in the kitchen —they must be cooking a feast.

He stood in the doorway, looking at them both.

"Tell Willie," he said, "I know who the murderer is and it's not him."

17

A reunion with his wife, a long night's rest in a bed he could call his own, the kids arguing over breakfast—it didn't take much for Dober to feel at home again. West Berlin was outside, but this was what mattered. He had lived half his life out of a suitcase; he had learned to appreciate the essentials.

In the afternoon, the whole family visited the city's zoo, one of the oldest in Europe; the kids had to be dragged away from the elephants and the dolphins. They had dinner in a restaurant on the wide, tree-lined Kurfürstendamm, the main boulevard of West Berlin. It was one of the few parts of the city that didn't lose all its life after sunset. The busy sidewalks and elegant stores, eating places, theaters, and hotels reminded Dober of Paris, and yet the style of the people, the architecture, the atmosphere was raffish and crudely unconventional in a uniquely Berlin way. Divided now for over thirty years, the city lived with a natural tension, not taking anything too seriously anymore, except the shortage of jobs.

As they went in the Burger King restaurant—get the kids ready for the burgers back home!—Dober noticed a little man with glasses trailing behind them. He'd first seen him when they began strolling on the Kurfürstendamm over half an hour ago. The man followed them into the restaurant and sat on the far side, reading a paper, as inconspicuous as possible. He irritated Dober—he was spoiling an innocent family occasion!

While they waited for service in the busy place, his wife talked enthusiastically about the Sunday morning Dixieland brunch at another restaurant on the Kurfürstendamm. She was as keen here as she had been in Poland to take the kids anywhere that imitated home, as if inoculating them against foreign influences.

"Let's check it out next Sunday," Dober said cheerfully, all the time watching the man who was observing him. It hadn't taken long for news of his arrival to circulate. He wondered who it was—the Germans? the Russians? He had been long enough in Poland to learn the different styles there, but not here.

"What's the matter, Frank?" He had missed something his wife had said and she followed his eyes.

"We're popular," he replied, grinning to reassure her.

"Who is it?" she whispered while the kids were distracted by kids at another table.

"Just a routine surveillance. Probably the Russians. Nothing to worry about."

But she did worry. A shadow had fallen across their bright reunion. Throughout the meal, she was continually glancing across the restaurant. The little man must have realized he'd been spotted, for he eventually paid his bill in a hurry and rushed out. Dober examined each new arrival, wondering who the replacement would be. Finally he decided on a youngish man, lean and blond, who sat near the door with his back to them. Dober caught him eyeing them in the mirror with professional casualness several times.

Dober hoped the disappearance of the little man would relax his wife, but she remained tense, snapping at the kids, who were restless and noisy. Seeing his wound the night before had upset her; his offhand references to the job were no longer convincing—all her fears were justified now and growing. It was time they went back to the States, to a quiet, ordinary life, before the kids caught his tension, too. And soon they'd be able to do it.

He touched his wife's tense face with tender fingers. "Be happy," he said. "All this'll soon be over. It's only routine anyway. They think I must have come on some big important mission. Poland has made them jumpy. When they intercept Washington messages showing I'm just here on a routine temporary assignment, they'll lose interest. You'll see. I know how they operate."

It didn't satisfy her, but she didn't want to discuss it in front of the children. When they strolled back along the Kurfürstendamm, the lean, blond man was a few yards behind, like a status symbol in this strange city divided between East and West.

Dober felt like a quiet night alone with his wife—he'd been looking forward to the time the kids would go to bed—but she'd invited an old German woman in for supper, to watch a special TV program on Germany in the thirties. The old woman lived on a small pension, couldn't even afford a TV. Clara offered to phone the woman not to come, but he told her not to bother. The old woman had probably been looking forward to the program about the days when she was in her prime. She didn't sound too formidable, and she'd probably leave early. How wrong he was!

Big-boned, with cropped gray hair and a black lace shawl, the old woman had been a librarian until cataracts on both eyes forced her into retirement; now she gave all her energy to talking instead of reading. She kept referring nostalgically to "the good old days" in her heavy accented English. At first Dober assumed she meant the days of her prime as a head librarian and he listened sympathetically, but then he realized with a shock that she was referring to the days of Hitler.

The TV program about the thirties dealt more gently with

160

the Nazis than American TV would have done, but the old woman considered it very unfair and inaccurate.

"Nothing is all good—nothing," she said in her dominating way. Of course there were the concentration camps, she added, but they'd been much exaggerated by the Jews, and Hitler hadn't known about them until close to the end, when it was too late. She had a paranoid hatred of Communism and the Soviet Union; to her, the tragedy of World War Two was that Germany and America hadn't become allies against Russia. Communist propaganda against Hitler had been too clever!

"Such an alliance, I tell you, could have kept Germany free from Communism. Now look at what has happened. Your president says the Russians won't crush the Polish revolt. Ah, if they do not, it is because they have some trick up—how do you say?—their sleeve . . ."

Dober, playing the polite host, tried to get her talking about books, but a reference to Thomas Mann quickly took her back to Hitler again. He sensed that she wanted him to argue with her, to give her the chance perhaps to steamroll him in front of his young wife; but to him, she was merely an old woman with an obsession—what was the point of an argument? With each glass of heavy Rhenish red wine, she became more aggressive, but he deliberately avoided getting involved, lighting a cigar and puffing out a barrier of smoke, reminding himself of the director—perhaps her argument would have appealed more to the director, because he was willing to stomach any kind of allies against the Russians.

He was relieved when Mills arrived unexpectedly and asked to speak to him privately. He could leave the old bitch then to Clara, who had befriended her because she seemed lonely. You might just as well befriend a monster.

"This is the first time she's ever got like this," Clara whispered apologetically. "It must be the wine."

161

"Don't worry about it." His wife's helpfulness to strangers used to irritate him. Now he rather admired it and felt the lack in himself.

He took Mills into the kitchen and closed the door. They sat around the big kitchen table with a bottle of Scotch between them. On the wall was a color photograph of the president, another of Clara's inoculations for the children.

"Do you think he'll be reelected?" he asked as Mills remained silent.

"I hope so. He's backed us. It'll be good for the Agency." Mills added abruptly, "How long have you known her?" He gestured toward the dining room.

"The old woman? I just met her this evening."

"How did your wife meet her?"

"They got talking in the park. You see how she talks!" He realized Mills was asking too many questions. "Why?"

"She works for the East Germans."

"That old monster? You sure?"

"We've got a file on her."

Dober grinned ruefully. "They're giving me a lot of attention. I was tailed today."

"They've done the same with Hinds in Madrid. A girl he picked up—who picked him up—worked for the Russians."

"The only connection between Hinds and me is the Ivan affair."

"Sure, they're nervous."

"Why?"

"Search me."

"The old monster in there brought up Poland, wanting a reaction from me. What's happening in Warsaw now? That's the key."

Mills said slowly, "The government is stalling. The negotiations between the workers and the government are dragging on. The government's using all kinds of delaying tactics, almost as if they're playing for time. The Roman

162

Catholic leaders are taking a strange attitude, too. They've eased up on their attacks on the government."

"Maybe they don't want to upset the negotiations. The church-government relationship is still the most sensitive barometer of the situation in Poland."

"It's almost as if . . ." Mills frowned, searching for the right words. "Some of the Roman Catholic statements urge the workers to relax their demands, to meet the government halfway."

"I tell you, it's part of that sensitive, subtle relationship between the state and church in Poland, unique in the communist world—"

"No, Frank, it's more than that. It's as if the Roman Catholic leaders are preparing the workers—not for compromise even, but for defeat!"

"That can't be. No, Mills, that's wrong," Dober said, getting up restlessly and leaning against the large family-size refrigerator. "How can they lose now?" Mills didn't understand Poland. Here in Berlin, he was too far from what was happening. He was as out of touch as those darned analysts in Washington.

Dober moved toward the door, suddenly concerned about his wife. "How am I going to get rid of the old monster out there?"

The two women were chatting harmlessly over coffees and liqueurs. Seeing the aggressive old woman now, Dober wondered why he hadn't spotted her at once. Her talk, her anti-Communist smoke screen, should have been a giveaway. Of course one ran into so many Nazis still in Germany—God knows there were even some back home—that she'd sounded convincing. But he should have seen through her game. Maybe he hadn't because she'd come to him through Clara, where he was most vulnerable. It probably wasn't planned for her to penetrate the family circle. It was just a lucky break because she was pushy and Clara was sympathetic to

163

older people. Basically they were just checking on him . . . a routine surveillance, post-Ivan . . . there was no reason to be alarmed . . .

The missing clippings on Frances Cernik's list were from American newspapers and magazines over thirty years old; several were no longer in business. The newspaper library on West Forty-third Street had some of them on microfilm, and Henrik spent several hours threading film through a viewer.

It was dull, monotonous work, and the World War Two headlines flashing by made him nostalgic for better days. He had been in his prime against the Nazis, sure of Estonia's future and his own after the war—somehow the Russians would depart for good and once again his little country would be independent, with him prominent in its government. Ah, what dreams! The Russians had stayed, and the future instead found him in America, here in this library among the researchers, to whom those days were no more than a roll of film, the future prime minister no more now than Farel's legman.

Bah, stop being sentimental! Henrik told himself and tried to concentrate on his search. At last he was successful.

The clippings concerned a series of eyewitness descriptions of the Auschwitz camp, where thousands of Polish Jews and others had been killed. Many of them had been used like animals for experiments in the medical barracks before being taken to the gas chambers and the ovens. There were detailed accounts of the cruelty of the guards and the doctors. It must have been a shocking revelation for many American readers at the time the articles were published, Henrik thought, but probably a lot of them didn't believe it.

He read carefully through each article, wondering what in it might relate to the murder of Ursula Rogal—if anything did. Farel would know.

He had copies made of each one to take back for Farel to

164

read. More for the files, he thought gloomily on the way to the subway, and they were already overcrowded.

Back at the apartment, he found father and daughter in the middle of one of their infrequent arguments.

Virgie appealed to him. "Henrik, Leo knows who the murderer is and he won't tell me. Isn't that unfair?"

"Virgie," Farel said sharply, "I'm sorry now I ever mentioned it. I can't possibly accuse someone by name until I'm completely convinced I can prove it to the satisfaction of the police. Henrik will tell you I'm the same way about my work. I never announce the result of my analysis until—"

"Oh, all right, Leo," she said disgustedly. "Keep your little secret."

"It may not be for long." Farel smiled disarmingly at his daughter. "What Henrik has brought me may be what I need."

"I doubt that," Henrik said cautiously.

"Let's take a look."

They retired to the Ivory Tower. Farel laid the copies out on his desk and read quickly through them.

"Thank you, Henrik," he said, sitting back. "We know Miss Rogal was in Auschwitz after her imprisonment in that camp ten kilometers from Lyuboml. Yet if the clippings are relevant, they must also concern the killer . . . and his motive. The motive is the key that will unlock everything. But I haven't enough evidence yet to be sure of my conclusion."

For the rest of the day, he concentrated on Soviet affairs. A pastoral letter from the Polish bishops disassociating themselves from the Workers' Leadership Committee particularly interested him. "They know something," he told Henrik. "They're keeping their distance. That way the Soviet army won't have any excuse to attack the Church. The Catholic Church has learned the technique of survival over two thousand years. The Soviet Union as an enemy has nothing on the ancient Romans." He rubbed his eyes wearily. "As

165

soon as the election's over tomorrow, we'll get the proof I'm waiting for."

Henrik wasn't sure whether he was referring to the Polish situation or the Rogal murder.

Election day was gray and wet; it seemed to reflect Farel's mood.

Virgie at breakfast made the mistake of asking him whom he was voting for, and he replied with a long lecture on objectivity. Analysts couldn't take sides; political scientists—and kremlinology was the highest form of political science—should be detached from their subject and therefore they shouldn't vote.

Virgie noted that her father was very tense as the time for the testing of his analysis approached. She had a holiday from school, and so she decided to get out of his way. She went off to find out if the Museum of Natural History was open on election day.

Farel played restlessly with the TV, seeking some early election news—he saw the president on the way to vote, beaming with confidence, that was all—and then he went up to work.

Henrik arrived late, having stopped to vote.

"You better tell Virgie," Farel grunted. "She'll want to know your choice."

"It's private," Henrik said stiffly. "That's why it's a secret ballot."

"Don't tell me. Tell her."

They didn't speak again for several hours. Farel discovered two inconsistencies in recent Chinese statements that supported the idea of another struggle for power in Peking, and he began to go through the files in search of other recent clues he might have missed. But his attention kept wandering back to the pile of Soviet clippings to check nervously that

166

nothing had appeared at the last minute to challenge his analysis. Nothing had.

The election was neck-and-neck right to the end. Neither candidate had a clear majority of electoral college votes until early next morning. California at last put the president over the top, though he won that huge state by only a few thousand votes, and there were immediate calls for a recount. At dawn the president's opponent still hadn't conceded.

Farel went to bed but couldn't sleep. Virgie heard him getting a glass of milk in the kitchen and then going up to the Ivory Tower again. He didn't appear for breakfast, but he came down for lunch. By then the president was giving a victory grin on TV. He had won apparently by just over a hundred thousand votes. Perhaps the success of his Polish speech had made the difference. How ironic that would be —to win with a speech that would soon be proved wrong!

How soon?

He waited for the phone to ring.

It rang only once, and then it was one of Virgie's school friends.

Silence.

Where are you, Bruno?

He waited . . . and waited.

By late afternoon, he called the State Department. Bruno was just leaving.

"No news yet, Bruno?" He tried not to sound anxious. "Nothing from aerial reconnaissance or ground intelligence?"

"Everywhere's peaceful," Bruno said jocularly. "We've just heard that Moscow's responded warmly to the president's reelection. Tass is circulating several favorable official comments. They'd hardly do that if they were going back into Poland, Farel!"

"The two aren't necessarily related," Farel said somberly.

167

"Poland to them is an internal matter. They probably do welcome the president's reelection because they've dealt with him already. They've never dealt with his opponent. Better the devil you know than the devil you don't."

"Oh, come on now, Farel, admit when you're beaten. Be a good sport. You're out of luck this time."

Farel frowned with annoyance at Bruno's describing analysis in terms of luck—as if it were a game of tennis! Steady, he thought, Bruno's only trying to rile you.

"You should concede, Farel, like the president's opponent."

Bruno was enjoying his embarrassment. The State Department wasn't involved now; Farel was on his own . . . an outsider . . . a losing competitor. His failure would teach the State Department and the president a lesson for consulting an outside analyst and not depending on their own staffs. Farel understood the rivalries involved. And Bruno was also no doubt pleased for another reason: the president's reelection meant there would be no shake-up at the State Department.

"Call me as soon as you hear," Farel told him obstinately.

"Forget it, Farel. You know as well as I do they'd have made their move by now if they were going to."

"It's puzzling, but there must be an explanation. The delay—"

"Admit you're wrong this time and relax. Better luck next time. No harm's been done, thanks to the CIA." It didn't even hurt Bruno now to give the CIA some credit. They all must have made some deal under the federal umbrella. . . .

Farel hung up on Bruno's condescending voice. He caught Virgie watching him with concern.

"Well, if I'm wrong," he told her, "at least it'll mean there'll be no bloodshed in Poland. No more lives will be lost."

Virgie didn't know what to reply—she felt very inadequate. Her mother would have known just what to say to calm him down, to soothe his pride.

He went up to the Ivory Tower, not to work but to be alone. He told Henrik he could leave early. The Tass reports were just coming in over the teletype machine. He barely glanced at them—the Soviet chief of state had sent the president a congratulatory message, expressing confidence that joint efforts by the Kremlin and the president's administration could open the way for "considerable progress in the relations between the two countries"; a leading Soviet specialist on American affairs declared in an interview circulated by the Soviet news agency that the president's campaign speeches about limiting the world's armaments promised well for a positive foreign policy. The Russians were being as friendly as possible.

Meanwhile, Henrik and Virgie talked over cups of tea—Indian tea.

"It begins to look bad," Henrik said. She should be warned—the poor child had to live with Farel.

"Leo can't be wrong."

"No one is perfect, Virgie."

"But he is so sure. Leo never feels that way without good reason. You know that yourself, Henrik."

"Ah, you worry too much. At your age you should be happy. You will have enough worries later—when you marry."

"I'm not a child, Henrik."

He sighed. "No, you are Leo Farel's daughter."

18

Shortly after Henrik left, a cable arrived from Warsaw. Grotow reported that the Nazi specialist consulted by Ursula Rogal was named Rudolf Kraft; the relatives didn't know anything more about him.

Farel had heard of him. Rudolf Kraft was an old Jewish psychiatrist who had received a lot of publicity recently over the extradition of a New Jersey housewife wanted for Nazi war crimes in Austria. Kraft had tracked her down and then insisted on an official investigation, although he claimed it had taken years to persuade the government to do anything. Ursula Rogal had probably read about Kraft in the papers or seen him on TV, and then gone to see him.

Normally Farel would have left Henrik to follow it up, but he couldn't wait until Henrik returned in the morning. Kraft might have the evidence he was looking for.

Immediately Farel's weariness vanished. Immediate action was called for. He was at his best at such times. He found Kraft's number in the Manhattan directory and phoned him. A woman answered, middle-aged and abrupt, and she took a lot of persuading to bring Kraft to the phone. She seemed to think Farel was a neurotic patient trying to waste the doctor's time. At last she went away and soon a husky voice with a slight foreign accent came on: "This is Rudolf Kraft. What now do you want?"

Farel explained who he was and was about to say what he wanted when Kraft interrupted him. He never talked business on the phone. Farel must come to see him! "Make an appointment with my secretary for one morning next week. Until then I am very busy."

"This is very urgent."

"So are all my cases. I'm a very busy man. Sometimes I think everyone in this city wants mental hygiene."

"This concerns a murder—"

"That is the business of the police."

"—and Nazi Germany."

A pause, some heavy breathing, then a deep sigh. "Very well. Come to see me at once if you must. A matter concerning the Nazis cannot wait. It has already waited for too long —over thirty years."

Kraft lived in a brownstone in the East Seventies; he had a floor to himself. The front door opened on a small abstract waiting room, where the only sign of life was a busy fish tank. Beyond this was a large, untidy study with books and manila envelopes piled high on the floor. A middle-aged receptionist, dumpy and curt, left Farel to wait there. He stared round impatiently. The sense of disorder irritated him. How could anyone work there? "Nazi Atrocities" was scrawled in large letters on one of the manila envelopes; "Nazi Generals" on another. How could anyone think in this mess?

"Sorry to keep you waiting." A tall, thin, round-shouldered man with bushy white hair came loping in. He spoke quickly, nervously, towering over Farel. "A patient detained me. He's a well-known entertainer and he was threatening to commit suicide. I had to let him go on talking until I was sure he didn't mean it. Just a childish appeal for attention." He stuck out a long, bony hand. "I'm Kraft."

Farel's disappointment over the disorderly state of the room—a reflection of Kraft's mind!—was heightened by

171

Kraft's appearance. He looked too old to be of much help. They shook hands and it was like grasping the hand of a skeleton.

"Since we spoke on the phone, I've checked up on you, Mr. Farel. I know about Nazi-ologists, if there are such animals, but not kremlinologists. I understand you have a passion for facts similar to my own"—Kraft gave a dry, scholarly chuckle—"but we are interested in different fields. How can I help you?"

"I understand Miss Ursula Rogal came to see you some time ago."

The name clearly didn't mean anything to the old man. "I see so many people. Rogel, you say? R-O-G-E-L?"

"A-L."

"Do you know why she came?"

"I think she wanted to know if you could help her to trace the Nazi lieutenant who killed her father."

The long bony chin nodded. "Of course, Rogal! I remember now."

He went over to one of the piles on the floor and bent over, carefully searching through the tightly packed folders. That was probably how he'd become so round-shouldered, Farel thought. Someone ought to buy him a filing cabinet for Christmas. With a disgusted grunt, Kraft suddenly drew out a thin folder.

"Here it is—in the wrong pile! My German files sometimes get mixed up with my patients. Miss Rogal strayed among some of my schizophrenics. Perhaps my instinct told me that was where she belonged!"

"You thought she was mentally ill?"

Washed-out but still shrewd blue eyes studied Farel. "She was emotionally disturbed perhaps . . . unbalanced . . . I was aware of something wrong, but it was only a vague impression. I had only a brief conversation with her. I didn't examine her. But her attitude worried me. One learns to be suspi-

172

cious of people's motives in seeking revenge. An eye for an eye is justified in the Bible, but an obsessive, passionate desire for revenge after thirty years . . . Well, it worries me. It can do our cause more harm than good. A cool, calculating desire to see justice done even after all this time is a feeling I understand. It's one I share. But Miss Rogal, she went far beyond that. It seemed to me it was probably a substitute, an outlet for something else. She told me she'd spent part of her childhood in a camp. God knows what horrors . . ."

Farel told him of Willie's experiences with her, without mentioning the murder.

"Ah, yes, beating. The sadism, the masochism—marked for life! Poor woman. Outwardly she showed little of those years, except occasionally an obsessive glint in her eyes when she talked about the man who killed her father and her hunt for him. I didn't notice any of that sudden detachment that concentration camp victims often show, a hollow expression that sets them apart from other human beings. But there was something, I knew that."

The old psychiatrist spread out the contents of the folder —several letters and pages of notes—on top of a small rolltop desk.

"Oh, yes, I remember her clearly now. It was the notorious Lieutenant Anatole Bach who killed her father in Lyuboml. The lieutenant thought her father was Jewish! How's that for fatal proof that Hitler was wrong when he claimed you could look at someone and tell instantly if they were Jewish? I've got a bulging file on Lieutenant Bach, a choice sadist if ever there was one, an insult to the good name of Johann Sebastian Bach, my favorite composer. But I haven't yet located him. There were rumors he was somewhere in Utah, but I haven't found him. So I'm afraid I had to disappoint Miss Rogal. I still have no definite information for her."

"You don't know what's happened to her?"

"We haven't been in touch since."

"She's dead. She was murdered."

"Good God!" Kraft seemed genuinely shocked.

"It received a lot of publicity."

"I've been away—in Israel, collecting evidence against a former Dachau guard now living in Chicago. How was she killed?"

"Strangled."

"Has the killer been caught?"

"The police have arrested the wrong person."

"Where did it take place?"

"In her apartment." Farel briefly described the murder. When he reached the discovery of the body, the old psychiatrist was visibly affected. His eyes closed momentarily; his hands tightly clenched. "So she found out," he murmured. "She knew."

"Knew what?"

"The identity of someone I had tried to keep a secret." Kraft let out a long sigh. "I didn't know where Bach was, but one of the other people I was investigating was a neighbor of hers in the city—a man who had worked as a guard at Auschwitz."

Ah, it was becoming clearer.

"I made the mistake, I realize now, of mentioning it. It slipped out—usually I am more careful. She wanted to know who he was, what name he was now living under. She insisted I tell her. She became quite vehement, neurotically so. She had been in Auschwitz herself for a short time, and she had known this guard. Immediately he became more interesting to her than the missing Lieutenant Bach. I refused to give her any information. I hadn't got enough evidence against him. At Auschwitz, you know, they destroyed a lot of the evidence. There weren't many survivors. And I must be sure beyond any reasonable doubt before I tell anyone else, especially before I try to persuade the immigration authorities to take action. You understand? Sometimes you can

174

wait too long, amass too much evidence . . ."

"I know that feeling from my own work," Farel said.

"Perhaps I waited too long in this case. I might have prevented this murder if I had moved faster. But I like to find out first if they have tried to atone themselves for their crimes. If so, justice may already have been done. I don't believe in capital punishment. Never have."

"But Miss Rogal must have found out . . ."

"Why do you say that?"

"Because the man was one of those who discovered her body."

"Ah, you guessed that. Well, how did she find out? I certainly didn't tell her."

"When she was here, was the file on the Auschwitz man on your desk?"

"Yes, I was working on it when she arrived. That's why I mentioned it. It was on my mind. I should have kept my mouth shut. I usually do."

"How long was she here?"

"Maybe half an hour, Mr. Farel. She was very persistent."

"And was she alone here at all during that time?"

Kraft thought back. "Yes . . . for a few minutes. I have an old man's bladder. I went to the john."

"Long enough for her to look at the file on your desk and learn the man's name?"

"Oh, yes." Kraft leaned forward, nodding. "You're right. She was quite capable of doing that. And quite capable, too, of getting in touch with him and threatening to expose him. Perhaps she wanted him to beat her to make her masochistic nostalgia, her sexual fantasies, more real. It would not be impossible in such a case. Poor woman, she had an obsession that was very unhealthy. I wish I had had a chance to examine her and get to the roots of it. I suspected her intense interest in Lieutenant Bach was not only because he'd killed her father but because he'd ill-treated her—perhaps raped

175

her. But she shied away from it when I tried to question her. I lost most of my large family on both my father's and my mother's side in one camp or another, but I don't burn with the same spirit of revenge that she had. A little justice is all I seek—and I'm quite willing to show a little mercy! I've dropped several investigations because I found the people were living exemplary lives. I felt they had done their best to atone. This man I foolishly mentioned to Miss Rogal, I was still uncertain about him. But I was wrong. He hasn't atoned. He was still capable of killing her. Which was the greater crime—the murder of Miss Rogal or his work at Auschwitz?"

"Does it matter as long as he pays for one of them?"

"Oh, yes, there is a difference."

"Tell me." Farel was respectful now—it was a mistake to think of Kraft as old.

"The murder of Miss Rogal is merely a single murder. Punishing him for that is merely a lesson against murder in general. But tracking him down for his crimes at Auschwitz provides another example that wholesale murder doesn't pay, even at a government level. Governments still need to be shown that. That's why I'm not going to tell you the man's name—at least not yet. I must first think about it. If it would mean that he would escape his war crimes, then perhaps it would be better if I simply pursued my own investigations."

"It's too late for that," Farel said gently. "You see, I already know who he is."

Kraft obviously didn't believe him.

"The priest . . . Father Joyce."

19

Kraft stared at him, astonished.

"How did you find out?" The old psychiatrist gestured toward the files on the floor. "I know you didn't sneak a look. But it took me ten years of research to find him! I had to track him from Germany to Poland to Italy to Ireland to here."

"We approached him from different angles," Farel said. "You were concerned with his past. I was interested only in his present—the Rogal murder."

"What was his error there?" Kraft said eagerly, one analyst to another.

"One detail was wrong," Farel said thoughtfully. "One sequence of events didn't make sense."

"Do tell me."

"Father Joyce said he had an appointment with Miss Rogal at seven-thirty, yet a short time earlier when she met her friend, Frances Cernik, for cocktails, she was in no hurry and would have gone on drinking indefinitely if Miss Cernik had been free. It was possible she'd forgotten about the appointment, but not likely, as she was said to have originated it. The only other explanation was that Father Joyce had invented the appointment to explain his presence in the house. And if he was lying about that, perhaps he was lying about her request for religious instruction, too. Maybe there was something else between them—and my talk with you has suggested what that could have been. A doubt about Father Joyce was sown in my mind, and it made me scrutinize the evidence concerning him more skeptically."

Farel went on briskly, warming to his argument, "There was a sequence of events involving him that I realized didn't make sense. The old superintendent was quite definite that he saw three people enter the house and in the following order: Miss Rogal first, then Father Joyce, and finally Mr. Rivera. Father Joyce claimed he couldn't gain admittance to Miss Rogal's apartment, and so he should still have been outside the door when Mr. Rivera went upstairs. But he wasn't! Mr. Rivera said he saw nobody. Yet when Mrs. Charles shortly afterward looked out of her next-door apartment, Father Joyce was there. So apparently he was missing for a short time. Where was he? There is only one possible explanation. He was inside Miss Rogal's apartment. She let him in, he killed her, and in his panic ransacked the apartment for anything that related to his Nazi past. And then he came out, closed the door, and calmly pressed the doorbell as if he'd been doing it for some time. Mrs. Charles had heard him admitted, but she thought he was one of Miss Rogal's students who had come by earlier."

"He's a cool customer, all right," Kraft said. "That's typical of how he managed to transform himself from a Nazi at Auschwitz to an Irish-American Catholic priest here. His real name is Karl Randt. He was born near Munich and was old enough to take part in the invasion of Poland. I have his early life documented, but there's no reason to bore you with it now. I'm trying to telescope, to summarize the evidence I've collected, you understand. He became one of the hardcore Nazi staff at Auschwitz, responsible for selecting those to go to the medical barracks and the gas chambers. It's difficult to collect eye-witness evidence against him because so few survived Auschwitz. I have a statement from a woman

178

who witnessed him take her husband to the gas chambers, but it is unsigned and the woman has since died. I've also been promised another statement from a man now in Yugoslavia, who witnessed him pushing a line of prisoners toward the gas chambers, sometimes beating them brutally. But promises are sometimes not kept. People become nervous, afraid, even after all this time. There's a feeling that the Nazis still have powerful friends. Even in this country they are sometimes regarded as valuable anti-Communists, allies against the Soviet Union. Bah!" Kraft cried, gesturing angrily with his clenched fist. "That attitude makes me mad! Sometimes you get the feeling even our government isn't keen to act. The denaturalization process, the extradition—it can take forever even when the evidence is overwhelming. In this case, the evidence is not yet overwhelming."

"Your evidence seems more complete than mine," Farel said. "The old superintendent might not stand up to a tough police cross-examination. The motive seems clear, but it's still largely speculation. I doubt if it would convince the police yet to give up their case against Willie."

Kraft said thoughtfully, "My data is more complete on his post-Auschwitz, pre-Rogal period. After the defeat of Germany, he portrayed himself as a victim of Nazi political persecution who was interned in Auschwitz, and he sought asylum in Italy. The specifics of his story were never seriously examined. Many in the Italian Catholic Church were willing to make excuses for Nazis, provided they were against Marxism and the Soviet Union. One bishop, for example, ran a very effective postwar underground railroad for Nazis from Italy to North and South America. Our man was found a teaching position in a Catholic college in southern Italy, then after about a year he was transferred to Ireland to complete the final grooming for America. He told people in Ireland he'd been a lay brother in an Italian religious order for years. He'd learned to speak English—his very slight

179

guttural accent could easily be mistaken for the harsh Gaelic accent of many Irishmen, particularly from Belfast, I believe —and he'd also studied Catholicism. He became Brian Joyce and, while in Ireland, began to study for the priesthood. Someone in Illinois, who had known him in Italy, filed the necessary forms for his admittance as a displaced person to the United States in the spring of 1950. Like all refugees arriving under the 1948 Displaced Persons Act, he was interrogated by the Immigration authorities. The former Auschwitz man gave all the correct answers. The past was quickly rubbed out with a few ready lies backed up by his convincing documents and appearance.

"Once in America, he settled down to being Brian Joyce —Karl Randt was dead. He settled first in Chicago, where he completed his studies and was ordained a priest. He apparently did some good conscientious work among the poor and, since he moved to New York, he's continued to be a good conscientious priest. Everyone who has worked with him praises his devotion and his modesty. I've come across no dissenting opinions. That's why for the last year or so I've rather slowed down, dragged my feet. On the basis of the evidence I had, his religious conversion seemed to be sincere. I thought perhaps he had sincerely been trying to atone for the guilt of his past. But this murder upsets that idea. I suppose she threatened to expose him—to ruin Brian Joyce and send him back to being Karl Randt—and Jekyll became Hyde again. He reverted to his original nature, poor man . . ."

Kraft began to put the letters and notes spread out on the roll-top desk back in the folder. "I think my best course is to proceed with my researches. If I obtain the statement from the man in Yugoslavia, then I think I'll give the Immigration authorities all I have."

"I can't wait that long," Farel said. "I've promised to get Willie out of jail."

180

"Yes, I'd forgotten him," Kraft said. "The innocent, they've suffered enough." He put the folder absentmindedly down on top of "Nazi Atrocities." "Occasionally I haven't waited to collect all the evidence I needed. I've played on the person's guilt. If they're basically decent, it sometimes works."

"What do you suggest?"

"Something simple." Kraft sat down at the desk and scribbled briefly on a sheet of paper. "I suggest we put this in an envelope addressed to Father Joyce and, on the way home, you leave it in his mailbox. Then we sit back and wait for something to happen. If he hasn't reverted completely to his Auschwitz days, something will."

"What is it?"

The old psychiatrist held up the sheet of paper.

He had drawn a large swastika.

Farel took a cab across the park to the priest's house and told the driver to wait.

He couldn't get the envelope in the mailbox and so, unwillingly, he pressed the bell. It was a risk in case the priest answered—a confrontation might spoil it. But he was lucky. A middle-aged housekeeper, a plain woman with a friendly smile, opened the door. She took the envelope as if she were relieved he hadn't come with anything more serious, an SOS for money, perhaps, or help with sudden illness.

"Father Joyce is in church," she said. "I'll make sure he gets it as soon as he returns." She looked curiously at him.

"Thank you," he said and walked back to the cab. It was as simple as that.

Home now. The cab couldn't take him fast enough, rushing up Central Park West. He'd been gone a long time; he was impatient to get back to work.

The apartment door opened as soon as he stepped out of the old, noisy elevator.

181

Virgie was waiting for him.

"Mr. Bruno at the State Department has called several times," she said. "It's very urgent. Please call Mr. Bruno at once." Farel didn't look pleased, and she added firmly, "At once, Leo. I promised him you would."

"All right, all right."

As he walked to the phone, it began to ring.

"That'll be him again," Virgie said.

"Hello, Farel here."

"Did everything go according to plan, Mr. Farel?" It was Kraft.

"Yes, a housekeeper took it."

"Good. Now we just wait. Will you phone me if you hear anything, and I'll do the same."

The old psychiatrist sounded very confident—he might have been waiting for a time bomb to go off. Farel was less sure. The priest must be a tough, canny character; he wouldn't be trapped so easily. But anyway he had no more time to worry about it at present. He felt in a pleased way as if he had shifted some of the responsibility onto Kraft, leaving himself free to pursue the Chinese clues.

The phone rang again as he was going upstairs.

This time it was Bruno.

"Farel . . ." Bruno's voice sounded much more friendly, also less self-confident. "Farel, I've just called to tell you— you were right!" Bruno seemed hardly able to believe it; shock and confusion made his voice rise. "The Soviet army has crossed the Polish frontier . . ."

Farel slowly smiled. It was a moment of complete satisfaction.

20

The Soviet general, a sixty-two-year-old tank veteran of World War Two named Ivan Bunov, watched his armored columns speed down a Polish highway leading to Warsaw.

Action at last! All week General Bunov's army had remained under the most comprehensive camouflage, the most rigorous discipline, and the men were as restless as horses kept too long in the stables. The lumbering lines of tanks groaned and clanked on the road past him. Their formation was too orderly, but it didn't matter because there was no danger from the air. This wasn't a war. It was just a police action, putting down the rebellious Poles. Even now that he had received the long delayed go-ahead from Moscow, the politicians, the bureaucrats had given him no freedom to act. He was to move his army to the outskirts of Warsaw and the other Polish cities . . . and wait. The only activity in the air was to be reconnaissance.

Most of the Soviet troops who marched past him into the wagons and trucks and tanks were young and green. Only the oldest men, most of them officers, had had any real combat experience, and that was over thirty years ago against the Germans. Korea, Vietnam, Africa—new weapons could be tested there, but not your infantry. What his men needed to season them, to make them real soldiers, was a direct all-out confrontation with an enemy; he yearned for

183

real combat once more before he retired, like an old man longing for sex again before death. The younger officers coming up, the future generals, tried to give the impression that wartime experience wasn't necessary. They were more like technologists than soldiers, probably much more content commanding robots than men, convinced that detailed knowledge of missile weaponry was more valuable than guts under fire. Ah, wait until they experienced real combat!

The general knew, as precisely as if he were there, that his advance units were already drawn up outside the Polish capital near the site of an old Nazi concentration camp, but he had to see them for himself. Minutes later his helicopter was dropping down on a rough landing pad behind a line of artillery that, he thought proudly, could devastate the city. And if the new bombers could be added to the guns, no enemy could withstand such an assault from land and air, not even the NATO armies in western Europe or the Americans!

But it was another waiting game. He had waited all week to cross into Poland; now he was waiting again—this time for the order to go into the cities. If they could have struck here immediately, the Polish workers would have offered little resistance. But now the workers had been warned, and the latest reports described the barricades being built in the center of Warsaw. War today, he thought indignantly as he clambered out of the helicopter, was like fighting with one arm tied behind your back. Perhaps the younger men were right and it should be fought with robots and long-range missiles. Let the human beings stay at home!

An old colonel he had known ever since they had fought together at Stalingrad over thirty years ago joined him outside the helicopter on a grassy mound. A couple of KGB men stood a few yards away—the snoopers were everywhere. Warsaw was probably already riddled with them again.

"Who are those fools in Moscow waiting for now?" he

grunted, careful to keep his voice low. He, the commanding general, still had to be careful of what he said!

The old colonel smiled cynically. "They want the cake and to eat it, too, as the Americans say—to check the Poles and yet not antagonize the Americans. The harvest has been very bad; we shall have need of American grain. We're kept waiting here in the interests of détente . . ."

"Get me the file on Bunov," Farel said to Henrik as he studied the early news items.

"The Bunov file is waiting on your desk," Henrik told him with a pleased smile.

"Excellent, Henrik. I congratulate you on your powers of anticipation."

"Ivan Bunov" . . . it was a fat file. Bunov had been active in Soviet military circles a long time; he was surely over sixty . . . yes, sixty-two, according to the file. A World War Two hero . . . famous, like Patton in the U.S. army, for keeping in close touch with the front line . . . born outside Leningrad, his father a farmer . . . In the early days of the Soviet occupation, Bunov was quoted as saying he identified with the Polish farmers: "All that farmers want is to be left alone to get the most out of their land. It's the people in the cities who cause all the trouble with their frustrated, artificial way of life."

Bunov certainly had no gift for politics, which explained why he hadn't reached the top level of the Soviet hierarchy —he was still a field commander manipulated by the politicians back in Moscow. But selecting him to command this invasion could mean something, Farel thought. He was comparatively popular with the Poles, not the right choice for a ruthless suppression. Did Moscow hope for some kind of compromise? . . .

Farel pushed aside the Bunov file and picked up summaries of Polish government and Roman Catholic statements

185

about the Soviet invasion. Both were curiously mild—something was going on behind the scenes.

"Henrik," he said thoughtfully, "get me the files on Andrzej Brewski and Cardinal Bierek." Henrik didn't move. "Now don't tell me they're here on the desk, too."

"That is so," Henrik replied.

While the Soviet army waited outside Warsaw like an eagle about to swoop, inside the city an important meeting was being held in a secluded house in Old Town.

Two men sat alone, facing each other, in a room full of medieval furniture. They were meeting in a showplace, one of Warsaw's perfectly preserved medieval houses, because it was the last place anyone—but especially their own supporters—would have expected to find them. Only a few guards and aides had come with them, and they were all waiting in an adjoining room.

One of the men was Andrzej Brewski, the boss of the Polish Communist party, and the other was Cardinal Bierek, the revered Roman Catholic primate of Poland. They were normally enemies, though they had long ago realized there was little they could do about it. They had to coexist in their divided country. Mutual interest in keeping out the Soviet army was what had brought them together now. They had swallowed their differences in the hope of preventing a wave of violent Soviet repression and maintaining a limited independence. In a historical setting that was a relic of Poland's glory, they were meeting to try to settle the Polish future. It was not the first time Cardinal Bierek, a tall gaunt old man with cropped white hair, had acted as a spokesman for the workers in a private session with Brewski.

"I was misled by the Americans," the cardinal said. "They assured me the Soviet army wouldn't come back."

"No," Brewski, a small sturdy middle-aged man, said. "They fed the Americans a phony line to save trouble in case the American president was pressured into doing something stupid during the American election. Moscow planned all along to come in as soon as the American election was over. The situation was getting out of hand. They just won't tolerate another Czechoslovakia at present—no liberal government, no end to censorship. They'll only go so far, and the workers don't seem to realize that. The Soviet army delayed a few hours because the result of the American election was close and a recount was threatened for a few hours."

"That explains why the negotiations stalled, never really got started. You knew what was going to happen."

"Of course."

"So now we have the Soviet army on the doorstep. Are we going to see Warsaw destroyed a second time—first by the Nazis and now by the Soviet Union?"

"They're not anxious to go the whole way." Brewski gestured with a small, meaty hand—before his political career, he'd been a stone mason. "They've made the first move, that's all. It's up to the workers now to respond. If the workers go peacefully back to work, I think the Russians will agree to keep the status quo. They don't want a big international fuss. They're anxious not to antagonize the Americans and lose the grain they need."

"The Americans can do nothing directly to help us. They daren't risk a nuclear war, another Cuban missile crisis. Our poor country! It's our fate to be sandwiched between the giants—Russia and Germany for centuries, and now Russia and America."

"Whether we like it or not, we're on the Russian side," Brewski said. "Russia is next door, America an ocean away. We're part of the Communist empire. To survive at all needs continual compromise. The workers don't realize that. You, too, Cardinal, sometimes forget in your more idealistic moments."

"It's not idealistic to hope, Brewski. It's realistic. Polish

187

patriotism has always flourished at the bleakest times. This bleak time, too, will pass away if we don't lose our national character and weaken."

"It's such talk that makes the workers so obstinate, so hard-headed," Brewski said angrily. "Don't you realize that if they don't back down, the Russians will destroy them! I've tried to talk sense to them, but they won't listen. They call me a Soviet lackey! But sometimes when you deal with a giant, you have to talk humble so he doesn't eat you up. There has to be a go-between. But of course those fools don't see that!"

"The living conditions deteriorated too much," the cardinal replied calmly. "Inflation meant they couldn't afford to eat. What do you expect them to do?"

"To be patient. Otherwise they'll be destroyed."

"It's in both our interests to make sure that doesn't happen."

"Let's cut the cackle, Cardinal. Have you brought me an offer?"

"If you make the necessary concessions, then I think the workers can be persuaded to go peacefully back to work. Otherwise—no!"

"I've already made concessions."

"Too few too late."

"We're heeding public opinion," Brewski said angrily. "There are no problems that can't be discussed and solved in a democratic way. But this new Workers' Defense Committee is a disruptive influence. They appeal to emotions at this explosive time. They attempt to sow discord, and they're active allies of alien centers hostile to Poland. They've even defied the law by failing to register!"

"We disagree with you," the cardinal replied quietly. "Failing to get any response to their protests, the workers rioted against the crippling food price increases. You attempted to suppress them with the utmost police brutality,

188

and the Workers' Defense Committee was formed to aid all those you imprisoned, as you know very well, Brewski. Let's have a frank exchange here today, or there's no point in meeting. We have no audience here, unless you have concealed a microphone in this room."

"I deny the allegations of police brutality. The police had to put down the riots. A train was derailed, traffic was blocked, there was looting. The police had to restore order. But they didn't use guns, even though some of them were injured."

"The evidence of police brutality is overwhelmingly against you. But we haven't come here to argue about that. The point is whether your Communist government and the workers can reach an agreement that will keep out the Soviet army."

"The government mustn't seem to be giving in, to be weak. The Russians won't accept that. What are the terms they're asking for?"

The cardinal took out several typed sheets. "Remember, Brewski, the workers don't want to face Soviet tanks any more than you or I do. All they want is a reasonable settlement between fellow Poles."

"Read!"

The old cardinal put on his glasses.

"Item one, the food price increases are to be cancelled and a special panel, including representatives of the Workers' Defense Committee, will review prices, costs, and wages, and present new proposals. Item two, an unconditional amnesty for all people convicted or even suspected of having taken part in demonstrations against food price increases. . . ."

Brewski's face hardened slowly as the cardinal read out a long list.

On the way to an emergency meeting of the National Security Council, the President had a brief phone conversation with the Soviet ambassador. They had established a direct relationship over the last four years and the president could be blunt with him.

"You fellers have put me in a tough spot. I told the American people you were going to be sensible and stay out."

"You were misinformed," the Soviet ambassador said smoothly. A handsome, sophisticated man who was a favorite of Washington hostesses, he had been selected because he had a style attractive to Americans, but he could make no commitments of any importance without consulting Moscow. Sometimes his hearty manner could make Moscow's line seem more flexible than it really was, but the president had learned over the years to allow for this. The president noted now that Moscow, via the ambassador, was admitting the United States had been "misinformed"—it was almost like a confession. He listened carefully as the ambassador added, "The Polish situation was getting out of control. We couldn't let it continue and grow even worse."

The president replied bluntly, "I don't think the American people will be willing to accept a lot of bloodshed and harsh repression. I may be forced to take some kind of ruthless action. Congress may also kill the grain deal."

"We hope to avoid that. We recognize that you have to satisfy your constituency just as we have to satisfy ours. But we hope it will be possible for us both to do that without any confrontation."

"If you go into Warsaw and fight the workers, I can't promise anything. I'm sending a direct message to Moscow condemning the army's action and warning of the dangers of further action."

"Good. We've instructed the Polish government to make concessions. We hope further army action won't be necessary. We've made our point. We've shown the Poles they can only go so far."

"Do you expect the workers to back down?"

"If they can save face. They're not fools. May we suggest that you use your influence to get the Catholic leaders to persuade the workers not to press for the impossible in their negotiations with the government?"

"We've already been in touch with the cardinal in Warsaw. He's got a list of the workers' demands. He considers them reasonable."

"What seems reasonable to the Catholic Church may not seem so reasonable to the government."

"I think the cardinal was speaking more as a Pole than as a Catholic."

"If the workers and the government reach an agreement, we'll be satisfied and it seems to us you should be, too. Your voters will be convinced your tough attitude has kept us out of Warsaw."

"Let's talk again in an hour," the president said firmly. "By then it should all be decided—for better or worse."

The president hurried on to the Cabinet Room, where the National Security Council was waiting for him. Sitting forward in his high-backed leather chair, his gestures tense with urgency, he began by summarizing his talk with the Soviet ambassador. When he mentioned the ambassador's remark, "You were misinformed," the director of Central Intelligence cut in, "I have already started an investigation."

The president obviously didn't like being interrupted. He said sharply, "Post-mortems and departmental alibis can wait. We've got to make some quick decisions." He glanced at the secretary of state. "I'd also like to consult Leo Farel. Get him to come here as soon as possible."

"He may not be willing to come back. He wasn't too pleased with the decision the last time."

"He was quite right not to be. He was right and the rest of us were wrong. If necessary, I'll phone him myself. I owe him an apology." The president looked slowly round the table. "There's a limit to what we can actually do, but we can

191

make a lot of noise. Apart from a tough warning to Moscow, we can immediately beef up our army in Germany. Leak stories about alerting our tactical nuclear strike force there. Then here at home get several prominent senators in Congress to link Soviet actions in Poland with the grain deal. If the Soviet army fights the workers, no deal! No grain! What we've got to do, gentlemen, is to orchestrate all our efforts for maximum effect. Get at the Soviet Union from several angles immediately, all within the next few hours."

It was noticeable that the president addressed most of his remarks to the secretary of state and ignored the director of Central Intelligence. The balance of power had shifted already.

21

A phone call from Mills was the first indication to Dober that something was wrong. Mills wanted him to come to his office in the Trade Mission immediately.

"Won't it wait until tomorrow?" After a night of heavy rain, the Berlin weather had turned sunny, and Dober had taken a day off to go sightseeing with his family—a couple of museums and of course the zoo.

"I'm sorry, Frank. Orders direct from Washington. I'll explain when you get here."

Dober was irritated. His wife couldn't drive; their plans would have to be cancelled. I've become too domesticated, he thought wryly. The idea of returning home had corrupted him! Mills probably just needed some help in preparing a Polish report. He was their authority on Poland until he went home.

The sunny weather had brought out the Berliners. The Kurfürstendamm was crowded. Out of habit, Dober parked the car a couple of blocks from the Trade Mission and walked the rest of the way, though he knew he was wasting time. The Germans and the Russians probably photographed everybody who went in.

Mills was waiting for him. Mills's office was like Mills: very neat, very impersonal except for a framed family snapshot on a clean desk. Sitting near the window was a heavily

193

built, impassive man Dober hadn't met before, though he'd been introduced to all the Berlin staff the first day. The man's smooth, tough manner suggested an interrogator.

"This is Len Dixon." Mills didn't explain who Dixon was; his attitude was subtly different, less respectful. "Sit down, Frank," he said curtly and Dober realized something important had happened, but he still didn't appreciate to what extent he was involved. The last Polish news he'd heard gave no warning . . .

"How can I help you?" he asked quietly, facing Mills across the desk.

"Well, Frank . . ." Mills hesitated, glanced at Dixon, fingered a letter opener on the desk. "The Soviet army has gone back into Poland. They're already outside Warsaw."

"You're kidding!"

"No, it's been confirmed from several sources."

"The Russians must have changed their plans at the last minute."

"Impossible. You know as well as I do an operation like that can't be carried out overnight. No, we've intercepted several army exchanges—it's been planned that way all along."

"So Ivan was wrong," Dober said, shocked.

Mills stared hard at him; Dixon leaned forward. "No," Mills said, "Ivan wasn't wrong. What he told you was wrong."

Dober didn't follow at first. "You mean . . ."

"Washington thinks we fell for a Soviet plant."

"A trick," Dixon said. Was he from Washington?

Dober, his memory flashing back to the scene outside the church, said quickly, "But Ivan was shot! . . ."

"Frank," Mills said, "listen to me. As soon as we got the news, we started an investigation in Warsaw. Ericson talked to some of the people who witnessed the shooting. Most of them said nothing, but he had one lucky break. One of the

194

storekeepers comes from Lodz like Ericson—Ericson was at school with his son. After checking out Ericson, he was willing to talk. He saw Ivan carried into a car, and when they thought no one could see, Ivan was talking to the others and they were laughing. Someone gave him a puff on a cigarette. It was careless of them, but they thought they were unobserved, and they got away with it until now."

"They said Ivan died."

"We only have their word for it, Frank."

"The storekeeper must be mistaken."

"He swears it's true, Frank. Ericson backs him."

"Maybe the others were laughing." Dober tried to master his emotions. "They sometimes give a guy a puff on a cigarette before his execution. No, I don't believe it."

"I can understand that, Frank," Mills said sympathetically. "But that's not all. We checked on Ivan's woman—the nightclub singer. You remember her, don't you?"

Dober nodded blankly. "She's not easy to forget. Beautiful high cheekbones, a strong full figure," and suddenly he chuckled, releasing some of his pent-up feeling. "Ivan had good taste . . . in women."

"Well, when we checked, she was no longer in Warsaw. She left two days after the shooting. A neighbor said two Russians in uniform came for her."

"To take her to prison. The traitor's girl—it fits."

"No, Frank, it doesn't fit. Her mother has received money from her. Can you send your mother money from a Soviet prison?"

"You're suggesting she's with Ivan?"

"It seems possible."

Dober got up and looked out of the window—to hide his face. The sun glinted on the traffic below; it all now seemed to have a sinister look. Mills and Dixon exchanged glances behind his back.

"What do you want me to do?" Dober said at last.

195

"Washington wants you to take a polygraph test."

"What?" Dober swung round, appalled, angry.

"You know how it is, Frank," Mills said apologetically. "We've been fooled. They want to check everything—everybody."

"That's not it," Dober said bitterly. "Washington's looking for a scapegoat." The president had been embarrassed; the director would be up for the ax unless he came up with a scapegoat very quickly. It had to be somebody senior. Dober was the logical choice as the station chief involved.

"Just a routine security clearance," Dixon said.

They took him to a room on the floor above, where a standard government leather easy chair was backed up to the familiar desklike construction, with the built-in apparatus of dials, graph paper and odd, narrow, metal pens.

Dixon told him to sit down in the easy chair and began to fit the three parts of the polygraph to him—the blood pressure cuff to his arm, the rubber tube around his chest, and the hand instrument to his palm. Dixon checked the three metal pens to make sure they would record any physiological changes—in pulse and blood pressure, breathing rhythm, and perspiration—on the moving graph paper. Dober was then hooked into the machine, told to look straight ahead at the wall and to be very still, and to answer only yes or no to each question, as if he were a novice and had never been through a lie detector test before. It made him even more uneasy.

Dixon stood behind him looking at the machine as he began to ask the questions—the usual general unrelated questions to start with to test reactions, such as *Did he smoke?* Dober replied to the blank wall in front, wishing he could see the machine's reactions. However certain you were of yourself, you were always unsure of the machine, and particularly so in his shocked state.

Dixon's questions ranged over his relationship with Ivan,

196

through all the stages of agent development and agent assessment. He asked about their meetings and the tradecraft involved to keep Ivan secure and free from discovery. When the interrogation reached the final meeting, Dixon asked variations of the same question, all the time watching the machine.

"You were sure Ivan had been shot?"

"Yes."

"Did you have any doubt he'd been shot?"

"No."

"Were you surprised Ivan had been shot?"

"Yes."

When Dixon finally released him, he couldn't read the result in the heavy, impassive face bending over him, but Mills who was standing near the machine looked relieved. Dober glanced down at the graph paper. The metal pens had maintained a steady progress.

"You're clean, Frank," Mills said. With a friendly smile, he added, "You understand, don't you? We didn't have any doubts, but we had to do it to satisfy Washington. They're panicking."

"I bet they are," Dober grunted.

Of course it wasn't a foolproof test. There were stories that you could train your mind to outwit the machine, although he had never come across anyone who had done it . . . except perhaps Ivan. Stefan had given him a polygraph test—or at least he said he had. Dober decided not to raise that. He'd think about it later when he was alone and more clear-headed, and he could pick up the pieces.

Mills told him to stay at home until they called him. Another car followed him home. Normally he'd have assumed it was the Germans or the Russians, but now he wondered if Mills had put it on him.

His wife had left him a note—she'd taken the kids to a movie. He was relieved to have the place to himself. He had

197

a lot of thinking to do—about the future as well as the past. He opened a bottle of Scotch, but in the act of filling the glass, he was suddenly lost in brooding and he put the bottle down again, unaware of what he was doing. The promotion to Washington could easily be lost now if the investigation found him negligent or guilty of faulty judgment. Was it really possible that the Russians—that Ivan—had faked the whole business? Not only was it possible, it seemed sure. Then to what extent was he to blame?

Dober sat in the dark lounge without even bothering to switch on the light, remembering all his doubts: he hadn't accepted Ivan for a long time; the church meetings had taken place only after weeks of checking. Stefan had finally convinced him with the polygraph test, all the other tests, even the tapes from the nightclub singer's bedroom, although her evidence wasn't worth much if she'd really been in love with Ivan, and a genuine love affair seemed likely if Mills was right and Ivan had arranged for her to follow him to wherever he was now—in the Soviet Union? Even double agents made the error of getting stuck on a woman. Dober thought guiltily of his own domestic happiness that was threatened now.

He went back methodically over his meetings with Ivan. If it had all been a Soviet game, how cleverly they had appealed to his prejudices! He had a man of action's, a puritan's, distrust of art and artists, and so casting the traitor as a cultural attaché—and a gambler and a womanizer—was shrewd. Even the meeting place was lulling. A cultural attaché in a Catholic church—weakness piled on weakness, "decadence," as the Russians would say, on "decadence." Who wouldn't have believed in a traitor in that setting?

Yet each time he thought of it as a Soviet game, he remembered Stefan. Stefan had spotted Ivan, had tested him thoroughly, had passed him and recruited him. Stefan held the key to the whole affair . . . and Stefan was dead, no doubt

198

of that anyway. He'd seen the body; he'd attended the funeral. Stefan had been shot in the back and his face in the coffin still had a surprised look. It was a very cold fall day —the bad weather started earlier in Poland than at home— and all the mourners were hidden in heavy winter clothes. Stefan's sister, a small ashen-faced woman with shoulder-length black hair, played Chopin's patriotic polonaise on the church organ, her tears dropping on the keys. He had tried to speak to her at the graveside while the diggers were shovelling in the frozen earth, but she had brushed past him, angry-eyed, and had walked away with an old man with a ruddy face in shabby mourning clothes. Surely she couldn't have known that he'd let her brother go to his death, and yet remembering those angry eyes now, he felt sure she knew something. He didn't doubt Stefan—that was unthinkable. Stefan had been with them too long, soon after he came out of his long tunnel of despair after Auschwitz. He'd been a boy in the resistance and the Nazis had eventually caught him and sent him to Auschwitz, but luckily Auschwitz had been liberated soon after and Stefan had been among the few survivors. Stefan had also passed not one but several polygraph tests, the last one supervised by Dober himself. But that wasn't it. Ivan had passed a test, too. Stefan had proved himself in action too many times over too long a period. No, he didn't, couldn't doubt Stefan, but the investigation would have to inquire into Stefan's relationship with Ivan, and perhaps his sister, his angry-eyed sister, could supply some of the answers. But Mills and Dixon wouldn't be that thorough—it wasn't their job on the line. He had to see her himself, and that meant returning to Poland, whatever the risk.

He drove downtown to talk to the Polish group—their cover was an import-export company—who had helped to get him and Hinds out of Poland. Much to his surprise, they readily agreed to get him back to Warsaw—no problem! The

Soviet army hadn't yet sealed off the frontier; trains and trucks were still getting through. He wanted to go as soon as possible before Mills heard of it and stopped him, so he arranged to travel with a consignment of food that night.

Clara and the kids were already home when he got back. The kids were watching TV—how pointless it seemed to protect them from reality when they got it on TV anyway, or maybe it just seemed like romance on TV. Scenes from Poland flashed on the screen—glimpses of Soviet tanks and a Soviet general. He told them he was going away for a couple of days on a routine mission. His wife, her eyes on the Soviet army massing outside Warsaw, gave him a knowing, anxious look, but kept quiet because of the kids.

"Will you be all right?" she whispered at the door.

"It's just routine," he whispered back, kissing her on the cheek—the lips might give away his own anxiety. "No talking to any more retired librarians while I'm gone."

She shook her head, giggling. She didn't have time for any more—the kids were pulling at him. Their goodbye was casual, though as he drove away he regretted not levelling with her. It was too late. Her future was at stake as much as his own. But he never had levelled with her, not until a mission was all over. What good would it do? he consoled himself.

The train journey was slow and uncomfortable, but also uneventful. They were stopped at the frontier and then again outside Warsaw, but there was no trouble, just routine inspections. The Soviet army wasn't ready yet to strangle the city. It was only when he left the station in a truck and travelled through the center of Warsaw that he saw all the potential danger. Warsaw already resembled a besieged city, with whole streets blocked off and workers building barricades and tank traps and training each other in the use of guns and home-made bombs—some of the houses must have been like armament factories. Walls of sandbags were going

200

up in front of key buildings. It looked heroic—and hopeless. The giant was outside the city waiting to strike; the Soviet tanks and artillery would rip through the barricades, the arms of the workers like peashooters against King Kong. Dober wondered why the Russians were waiting, giving the workers time to organize. Something was going on behind the scenes; the workers in the front-line were merely pawns; perhaps there was hope in being of no importance . . .

They took good care of him: the truck left him outside her apartment building in Ursus, a suburb that had been the scene of some of the fiercest demonstrations. The barricades were going up there, too. A car passed with boxes of rifles strapped to the roof. The driver looked like a boy, not even old enough to be an apprentice. The air was full of dust, as if the deposits of centuries had been disturbed.

Hoping he didn't look too conspicuous, too American— he had put on his plainest clothes—Dober walked casually into the apartment building, a typical concrete workers' block without frills. He knew she was a music teacher, and so when he heard a piano in the distance, he followed the sounds until he reached the right door. The piano kept starting and stopping as if a student were going through a lesson.

The door opened at his second ring and she stared out. Her eyes flashed when she recognized him, and the door began to close.

"I've got something urgent to ask you," he said in his clumsy Polish. She hesitated and he added quickly, ". . . about your brother—Stefan."

She studied him as if deciding whether he was telling the truth, and then she held the door open. "Come in." She seemed very tired and nervous—probably no one in Warsaw had had any sleep for days. She appeared much older than when he'd last seen her at her brother's funeral; her long dark hair was beginning to gray. "You'll have to wait until I finish the lesson."

201

Her apartment was one big plain room with a kitchen at one end and an old grand piano at the other. The player Dober had heard was a very serious youth who was bending over the keyboard trying to perfect a difficult passage—he might have belonged to a different world from the streets outside preparing for war. As she showed the youth where he was going wrong, playing the chords over and over again, Dober tried to learn more about her from the personal objects in the room. There weren't many: a statue of Christ showing the wounds; a bust of a young man with long flowing hair—was it Chopin?; a big, framed, yellowing photograph of an angelic boy in a dark suit . . . They didn't tell him anything he didn't know already. Who was the boy in the photograph? Had she been married? Was that her son?

The youth played through the piece again and stumbled over the same passage. Her patience ran out. "Practice it on your own," she cried at him, tense with Dober there and taking it out on her student. "And come back with it perfect!" The youth glanced at Dober, embarrassed. "Come, the lesson is over." She pushed him to the door.

"Shall I come at the same time tomorrow?"

"Of course . . . if we're all still here." She put a quick hand on the youth's shoulder. "I'm only joking. It's important to carry on as usual. Your music will be here after they're gone."

She stood at the open door watching the youth walk away. She seemed unwilling to face Dober. "Now what do you want?" she asked at last.

"To talk."

"I've got nothing to say to you."

Dober gestured at the yellowing photograph, partly from curiosity, partly to fill the silence. "Who's the young man?"

"You don't recognize him?" Her tone was bitter. "That's Stefan—when he was eleven. The picture was taken in Zelazowa Wola. We went to see Chopin's birthplace. In those days he wanted to be a musician or a priest."

Dober was astonished. There was no resemblance between the boy and the wasted, cynical man he'd known.

"The war changed him," she said. "Auschwitz. Without that experience, he would never have worked for you. He'd still be alive. He wasn't interested in politics until then." She rubbed her eyes wearily. "I shouldn't really be so angry with you. You were just the instrument. The Nazis really killed him—killed the spirit of the boy up there."

" 'The instrument'?—I don't follow."

"Well, you were."

"The instrument for what?"

"Oh, don't try to fool me now," she said angrily. "You had him killed."

"The Russians killed him," Dober said uncomfortably. She was probably referring to his silence, the fact that he hadn't warned Stefan. "We had a Russian informer. We called him Ivan . . ."

"I know all about Ivan," she said.

"Did Stefan tell you everything?"

"I think so."

"He shouldn't have."

"He had to trust someone. He was safe with me. He knew that, and he wanted someone to know the truth . . . in case anything happened. He knew something would happen sooner or later. That double game is too dangerous. I told him he was a fool."

"You talk as if I know all about it."

"You do. That's why you had him killed."

"You've got it wrong," and suddenly, impulsively, he told her everything up to his final meeting with Ivan.

She listened in silence; she seemed shocked.

"You're telling me the truth?" she said at last.

"What I heard, what I saw."

She looked at him. "So you don't know?"

203

"Know what?"

She sat at the piano and absentmindedly picked out a few bars of the Chopin polonaise she had played at her brother's funeral. "Stefan said the Russians would never trust him. Ivan probably wanted him killed because he knew too much, to make sure there was no slip-up, that Stefan didn't break down and tell you."

"Tell me what?" he asked her bent head. He knew, but he wanted confirmation, to hear her say it.

"The truth about Ivan."

"Stefan recruited him, tested him, gave him a polygraph test . . ."

"No, he didn't."

"He told me."

"He may have told you, but that doesn't mean he did it."

Dober said quietly, "After all we'd been through, I felt I could trust him."

She stared up at him, her tired eyes showing some sympathy at last. "That was the trouble, wasn't it? You did trust Stefan." Again she played a few bars of the Chopin, as if to clear her mind; it had also been a favorite piece of her brother's. "You must understand him. You—I—can't imagine what he went through at Auschwitz. Years later he still had nightmares about it, calling out the names of the guards: Franz Hubertz, Karl Randt, Richard Manheim . . . After his sufferings there, all those horrors he experienced—and remember he was hardly more than a boy—he became intensely political. He no longer had any interest in religion, in music—they were all 'luxuries.' He eventually joined you because he believed you would ensure Poland's independence. But after Hungary and Czechoslovakia, when the Soviet Union ruthlessly put down the uprisings and you did nothing about it, he grew bitterly disillusioned. He came to believe that Poland would never shake off the Soviet Union. America would certainly never risk a world war over Poland.

204

So on the old principle that if you can't beat them, you join them, he did just that."

"You're telling me that Stefan . . ."

"He double-crossed you. Yes! He changed sides! He was working for the Russians! I thought you'd found out and that was why he was killed and all the time it was them."

For a few moments Dober lost control. He cursed Stefan —"The traitor!" he shouted.

"Traitor to what?" she said sharply.

"I trusted him."

"In a game where there's no trust? You, too, were willing to let him go to his death. You told me so."

"I told you too much." He got up. "Ivan and your brother made up the whole thing between them. I don't believe it!"

"It's the truth." She played a few more bars of the polonaise—for comfort—talking quietly over the music.

"Stefan forgot his Polish history. He acted as if it was either or—either America or Russia. But a people that survives doesn't depend on a savior. They depend on themselves. Poland has always survived—we are a hardy people. We will continue to survive!" Her voice was harsh, her eyes gleamed almost fanatically. "Stefan had finally come to understand that. That was why he changed again and returned to his roots. He joined the workers. He had double-crossed you and at the end he double-crossed the Russians. He was on the workers' side. The Russians must have found out; that was why he was killed—because in the end he was true only to Poland and to himself!"

She softened the music as she told him, "Don't feel too badly about Stefan. He liked you, he really did. He said you were a man of old-fashioned virtues . . . in the wrong job. He certainly didn't spend the money you paid him on himself. He gave most of it away. You remember how badly he dressed; he ate in cheap cafés. It hurt him to have to play on your virtues. He and Ivan planned it all in great detail—they

205

decided Ivan had to die to make it completely convincing. You'd never question it then. It hurt Stefan, it really did, to deceive you, but he'd learned to separate his personal feelings from his political work . . . and of course he was the real loser. My poor dear dead brother!"

Her face bent over the keys again and the polonaise grew louder, more stirring . . . more mocking. Dober felt he couldn't stay there any longer with the patriotic music, the nail holes, the Chopin bust, the lost boy, the sense of betrayal. He walked quickly to the door and she let him go, but the music followed him all the way downstairs until he reached the street, and then the noise there of passing trucks loaded with guns at last drowned out the piano.

22

Father Joyce watched a wedding rehearsal in the church. It was to be a full-dress white wedding, with a church full of relatives and a reception in the church hall afterward provided by an expensive caterer. Everyone seemed so happy.

The smiling young couple coming down the aisle made the stocky, aging priest feel suddenly envious. They were Irish-Americans and they treated him like one of the family—a fellow Irishman—but he was aware all the time of the difference between them. He could never relax the way they could. It was still just a role to him, and recently it had become much harder to play. The Irish jokes, the Irish kidding, the Irish references, all the rest of it wearied him now. He listened to his own voice like an actor in a hit play hearing himself say the same lines for the thousandth time. By the end of the wedding rehearsal, he went back to the house drained of all his energy.

The envelope was beside the phone in the hall. He didn't recognize the handwriting and took it with him to his room to open later. It was probably a begging letter or a thank-you note—something that could wait. He felt too tired to be bothered right now.

He took off his jacket and his shoes and stretched out on the single hard bed. A piece of wood lay under the mattress to support his weak back, a memento of a boyhood skiing holiday in his other life.

He tried to sleep, but his mind was too active. For days now, it was as if the pattern of his life had been thoroughly disturbed, and all the pieces were out of place: he was no longer together.

He decided to open the envelope to distract his thoughts. It contained a single sheet of paper. He unfolded the paper and stared at the big crudely drawn swastika.

He stared at it for a long time.

Someone else knew!

He wasn't safe!

Trying to be calm, he examined the writing on the envelope. No clues. He carefully folded the paper again, replaced it in the envelope, and put it away in his pocket. Then he slipped on his jacket and shoes again and went down to the kitchen.

The housekeeper was relaxing with a bottle of beer and a *True Confessions* magazine. She was startled to see him. Her hands folded over the magazine's sensational cover. He spoke to her as if he hadn't noticed.

"That envelope you left for me . . . Who brought it?"

She gave him one of her friendly, disarming smiles. "A small man with a foreign accent. He didn't leave his name."

He thought about it for a few moments, remembering a TV program he'd watched recently.

"Did he have thinning dark hair and big eyes?"

"That's him. You know him? Is it important?"

"No." He turned away. "It doesn't matter," and he walked out before she could fire any more questions at him.

Leo Farel knew, he thought in a sudden panic. He had been uneasy ever since the visit of Farel's old assistant. A trip to the public library had shown him what he was up against. *Who's Who* had a long biographical section; he'd also seen Farel on TV. This was no obscure Polish schoolteacher.

To get away, he walked over to the church. No one was there at this time—the last of the wedding group had long since departed—and he moved restlessly back and forth past the Stations of the Cross on the walls. He couldn't kneel; he couldn't pray; he couldn't concentrate. It all now seemed part of the same act: the jolly Irishman, the pious priest. Father Brian Joyce was now being broken down, stripped gradually to Karl Randt again. Had he ever really changed? That sick blackmailing bitch had really been the past reclaiming him. One quick outburst of rage had wiped out the work of thirty years. God wants more in atonement from me, he told himself, feeling short of air, his mind reeling in the confinement of the church.

Outside an old wino tried to stop him—he was usually good for a quarter, kind Father Joyce—but he brushed past the battered old man as if he didn't see him.

He met the housekeeper leaving the house with a large shopping bag.

"What do you fancy for dinner, Father? Meat or fish?"

He hesitated. "It doesn't matter." She looked strangely at him. "I won't be here."

She waited for him to explain, then she told him sharply, "I'm glad I asked you. Food's too expensive now to waste."

She was genuine Irish from Galway and often tried to discuss the Irish troubles with him, but he discouraged her because he didn't trust her. But at that moment he would have gladly talked with her about anything, even Ireland. This was no way to be left, in silence, alone. She gave him no further chance, however, no last hope—his attitude had obviously offended her. She left him, slamming the door.

Well, maybe it was better this way, he told himself. He had made his decision. It had been made over thirty years ago. There was no escape this time.

He went in the sitting-room where a bottle of brandy was kept "for emergencies." This was an emergency; he downed

209

a wine glass full and then another—his nerves were jumping.

Then he went back to his room and locked himself in.

From underneath the bed, he took out the old Nazi SS uniform he had brought from Ursula Rogal's apartment in his briefcase (he'd also brought the files about Auschwitz. No clues to his Nazi past must be left there). He took off his clerical clothes, folding them neatly, although he would never need them again, and put on the uniform. It was too big for him, baggy at the shoulders and stomach, flopping over his hands and feet. But it transformed him. The last sign of Father Brian Joyce, of the last thirty years, of all his efforts, vanished; Karl Randt stood before the mirror, a seedy penitent. He hadn't feared God's eternal punishment, but punishment in this life—that explained the last thirty years. Was there no sincerity in Father Joyce? Was it all an act?

He stared in horror at the mirror and brandy tears ran down his cheeks at the sight of what he'd become.

He condemned himself.

He unlocked the faded old trunk that had belonged to his father—the trunk had survived the American air raid on Hamburg that had killed his parents. It contained his few mementoes that were anonymous enough to be safe. His hand, trembling slightly, rummaged under the family Bible, the family picture album, the sweater his mother had knitted for him the first year of the war, and at last he found what he needed—His father's old Luger pistol.

23

As soon as he saw who had come to meet them at Dulles Airport, Dober knew the worst. Lonegan was hardly more than a messenger.

Dober had already been told before they left Berlin that the director had resigned or been fired, and yet he still had hope for himself until he saw Lonegan waving genially from the barrier. It was the Agency's way of telling him he was through.

"Good to see you, Frank." Lonegan, small and neat, played his part well. Not a hint that he knew Dober was in trouble. While Clara rounded up the kids, Lonegan helped him to take their five pieces of luggage through customs. The rest was coming by sea.

"You know heads have rolled, Frank," Lonegan said carefully on the way into Washington. "The director, the deputy —My God, a clean sweep."

"And me next?"

Lonegan laughed, embarrassed. His instructions were to leave them at a midtown hotel. Dober was to do nothing but wait.

Two days went by without any news. He sent Clara and the kids out to see the sights. The White House, Congress, Lincoln Memorial, Washington Monument, the Kennedy grave—it was like an indoctrination course for the kids to leave Europe behind. Clara wanted him to go with them, but he insisted he had to stay near the phone. He sat watching TV and drinking Scotch. The second day, he began to snap at Clara and the kids—maybe he should pack them all off to her mother's until he came out of his depression. It wasn't so much the sense of failure as the cause of it, Stefan's double-cross. He'd known Stefan a long time, he kept telling himself, considered him a friend, mourned him, and yet all the time Stefan was . . . He still couldn't accept it.

Most of the TV programs were like blurs—he was more interested in the Scotch; but something caught his attention about a priest found shot in New York—he was wearing an old SS uniform. Catholicism and Naziism were an even more bizarre combination than the Polish brand of Catholicism and Communism. Curiosity made him listen to the details, and suddenly he was leaning forward to turn up the sound. The priest's real name was Karl Randt; he'd been a guard at Auschwitz. Dober wondered where he'd heard that name before. His memory toiled back and forth until he found it. Of course! It was one of the names of the Auschwitz guards Stefan's sister had quoted from Stefan's nightmares. But that wasn't all. What aroused Dober's suspicions even more was that a suicide note had been left by the priest, Karl Randt, addressed to . . . Leo Farel!

Farel!

It could only mean that the suicide had some international political significance. And involving both Farel and Stefan, it must also involve the whole Polish business. Perhaps here was the final key to Stefan's betrayal of him.

Three hours later, he was face-to-face with Farel in the kremlinologist's apartment in New York.

Farel knew who he was and had agreed to see him immediately.

212

"Mr. Dober," Farel said politely, "I'm glad to have this opportunity of meeting you. We've both been studying the same Soviet problem."

"You've been successful, Mr. Farel. I failed."

"In the pursuit of knowledge," Farel said gently, "there's no success, no failure." He liked Dober's directness and professionalism; he also had the analyst's sneaking admiration for the front-line man-of-action. "How can I help you?"

Dober explained briefly about Stefan without giving away any Agency secrets; it was obvious, he added, that the Stefan affair in Poland must be related to this suicide in New York.

"Everything's related," Farel said thoughtfully, "but not always closely." He explained the reason for the priest's suicide and briefly described the Rogal murder. "He left a three-line note addressed to me confessing to the murder." Farel knew the note by heart: *Dear Mr. Farel, You are quite right—I am a former guard at Auschwitz. I killed Ursula Rogal when she threatened to expose me. I regret it and will have to do further penance. Karl Randt.*

It only added to Dober's suspicions. Ursula Rogal was Polish—it all fitted. What was Farel hiding?

"Nothing," Farel said firmly. "In your front-line work, you look for the logic of conspiracy, of spying, of double agents. Everything fits together neatly because it is manufactured by one side or the other. But we kremlinologists are much more at the mercy of the waywardness of life. Logic only goes so far before the element of accident, of coincidence, the basic life forces, take over. You would only be truly convinced, satisfied now if Karl Randt was Anatole Bach, the man Ursula Rogal was searching for; if your friend Stefan was her relative in Poland; if she perhaps had worked for the CIA or the Russians . . . But life only goes so far, and that is too far."

213

Dober said obstinately, "But I know, Mr. Farel, that you wouldn't have gotten involved in a local murder case if there wasn't some great political significance behind it."

"Ah, that's where you're wrong, Dober. Even we kremlinologists are human. But I can see words aren't going to convince you. Come," he said briskly, "I'll show you the evidence." He began to hurry Dober to the door.

"Where are we going?"

"To a basketball game."

Farel refused to explain and Dober didn't insist. He welcomed some action.

A cab took them in a few minutes to a local high school. Farel hurried him inside to the school's indoor basketball court, where a large crowd was waiting for a game to begin. Farel introduced a serious-faced young girl to Dober. "This is my daughter, Virgie, and"—Farel pointed across to the players—"there's the reason for my involvement in the Rogal murder case." A very tall black youth, flexing his muscles, waved happily at Farel and Virgie. Farel explained who Willie was.

"But that has nothing to do with Soviet policy toward Poland," Dober said doubtfully.

"Exactly. Its relevance for you, Dober, lies in the concentration camp link. Karl Randt, the Auschwitz guard, is the link, not the whole point. The concentration camp experience explains what happened to Ursula Rogal, how her psychological wounds eventually drove her into a situation where she was murdered, and similarly your friend Stefan's experience explains why he became an agent, a double agent, and finally a patriot. Understand the concentration camp represented by Karl Randt, and perhaps you'll understand your friend—you may even forgive him."

The game had begun; Farel's young daughter was standing on tiptoe, yelling "Willie! . . . Willie! . . . Willie! . . ." Her intense enthusiasm finally convinced Dober that Farel's explanation was true.

"I must get back to Washington," he said.

Farel walked with him to the street outside.

"I hope you don't feel you've had a wasted journey."

Dober shrugged. "I wished to check."

They shook hands. Dober got into a cab, grave-faced. Farel watched until the cab disappeared. He liked the idea that Dober had come to find out more about his friend and not merely to save his CIA career.

And perhaps Dober succeeded. Somewhere between leaving Farel and reaching the airport, his mood changed. At some point in thinking back over the meeting, he found himself no longer hating Stefan. The masochism of Ursula Rogal showed what the concentration camp experience could do to you. God knows what it had done to Stefan. What was it his sister had said? *It hurt Stefan, it really did, to deceive you, but he'd learned to separate his personal feelings from his political work . . . and of course he was the real loser. My poor dear dead brother! . . .* My poor dear dead untrustworthy . . . friend! . . .

Dober's depression slowly lifted, so that when he returned to the hotel and learned the news—that he was being retired, honorably with full benefits—he almost welcomed it. He accepted the principle of paying for your mistakes, and this had been a big, bad one, and he was going to pay dearly for it—had paid dearly already—but undoubtedly there were compensations.

Clara watched him nervously. When she realized he wasn't shattered, all her pent-up feelings rushed out. No more fears for his life, no more separations; they had enough money to live quietly—she made it sound like good news.

"I'll get into something, maybe teaching. The Agency'll help me. They'll have to." Dober grinned—for the first time,

215

it seemed to him, since the Ivan business had all gone sour. "I know too much about them." He felt as if he'd lost his professional paranoia; now perhaps his marriage would be free of it.

Farel went back to the game. The giant players—Willie seemed much smaller among his peers—were rushing down the court. The ball was passed to Willie and a second later was through the hoop. The crowd roared, Virgie high on her toes as loud as anyone. Farel had never seen her so relaxed and outgoing. She caught him watching her.

"Thank you, Leo, for freeing Willie to win his scholarship."

"All that was needed was what Willie would call a few assists," Farel said. He had read *A Key to College Basketball* in preparation for watching this game. "A man's guilt was too heavy for him to bear. But, Virgie, I'm a kremlinologist, not a criminologist. Don't let's get involved in any more murder cases."

"Okay, Leo," Virgie murmured, her eyes on the game.

The loudspeaker snorted like a gun going off and a voice roared, "Mr. Leo Farel is wanted on the phone! . . . Mr. Leo Farel . . ."

"Who can that be?" Farel said, annoyed. "Nobody knows I'm here—except Dober. Maybe he's calling from the airport."

He was gone a long time, but he came back smiling.

"It wasn't Dober, it was the White House. The Secret Service traced us here through the New York police, who knew Willie had his first game tonight. The president wanted me to know the Polish crisis is over . . . for the time being. The Polish government has agreed to a complete amnesty and to cut food prices, and the workers have already begun to dismantle their barricades."

"Oh, Leo, a happy ending."

216

"There are no happy endings—the Poles know that as well as anyone. So does an Estonian! The president wants me to have lunch with him tomorrow to discuss what's likely to happen next." He seemed pleased, but you could never be sure with Leo.

"And you're going?"

"I was tempted to say no—the Chinese need my urgent attention!—but I decided to be obliging."

"Now all we need is for Willie's team to win."

And it did.